SHIFTING SHADOWS

SHIFTING SHADOWS

DANIELLE FORREST

The Eternal Scribe Publishing
Indianapolis, IN

The Eternal Scribe Publishing
www.theeternalscribe.com
theternalscribe@gmail.com

Cover Design: Danielle Forrest
Interior Design: Vellum
Printing: IngramSpark

First Edition
Paperback ISBN: 978-1-950795-18-5
Hardcover ISBN: 978-1-950795-19-2
Library of Congress Control Number: 2022918050

This is a work of fiction. All elements in this novel are fictitious and not intended to reflect or mimic real-life. Any parallels are strictly coincidental.

PRONUNCIATIONS

- Surg - Surge
- Diehli - Day-lee
- Ateles - Ah-tell-ease
- Taln - Talon
- Eirse - Air-see
- Wesa - Wee-sah
- Krayvo Ansa - Cray-voh Ahn-sah
- Lycaon - Lycan

DEFINITIONS

- Dicero(s) - about 2 minutes
- Horo(s) - 50 diceros or 1 hour 40 minutes
- Erno(s) - 15 horos or 25 hours
- Morgo(s) - 25 ernos or just over 26 days
- Alo(s) - 10 morgos or just over 260 days

*E*irse could feel the cool press of the water against her skin. It was comforting, like an embrace. She opened her eyes. Endless silver-capped teal waters stretched out before her, eventually fading into darkness. The currents tugged her back and forth, and she kept herself in position with a few flicks of her webbed feet and a lazy motion of her arms. Her sails did much of the work as she relaxed in the water, enjoying a little time close to the surface. The sun's rays played with the shallow depths, creating art as they struggled to make their way deeper on this rare sunny day.

She sighed in contentment. She could stay like this forever. Unfortunately, no life was ever that simple. Sure, the Tursiops had created a way of life that was far simpler than most sentient species in the galaxy, but they still had the same basic needs. They still had a hierarchy of leadership and skilled workers. People still had to *work*.

That being said, she had a lot of time for playing and daydreaming. She had time each erno to relax and enjoy what the seas had to provide in leisure.

"Eirse, come on already!" her hunting partner called out from the distance. "I've been looking all over for you."

Some part of her tensed, like something terrible was about to happen. "Yeah, I'm coming." She turned away from the surface. Lifting her arms to catch the water with her sails, she propelled herself forward, easily reaching her fellow hunter. "I'm ready," she said as she stopped in front of them.

They laughed. "No, you're not. You don't even have a weapon."

Eirse shrugged. "Well, you have two, so it's fine."

"That's because I knew *you* wouldn't be prepared. You never are."

She shrugged again. They'd gone out on hunts many times before, and she couldn't deny they were right. She was happy to do her part for the community, but she often dragged her sails about it. She was a good hunter, but she almost always needed a little nudging to get started.

This erno was no different.

"Thanks," she said as she wrapped her fingers around the shaft of the harpoon. It felt good in her hand, smooth and sturdy. "Let's go."

Eirse took off into the deeper waters, where their ideal prey thrived. They had to stop from time to time to allow their eyes to adjust as more and more light was filtered out by the water. Soon, they could sense more from hearing, taste, and touch than from sight. They stopped as their toes touched against the seafloor, and because they could not longer rely on their eyes to navigate efficiently, they focused on the flow of water over their skin, searching for the telltale way currents shifted around objects. They preferred places that gave them an easy out in case a predator came along, while also allowing them to scout for prey and throw their harpoon without interference.

Usually, the best places were against rock formations. Because the currents tended to run along the rocks, you could lean up against them, and other sea creatures might not notice your presence. Coral, on the other hand, was dangerous. It could be razor sharp and venomous. Vegetation was also a hazard, as it could snag you at the wrong moment. She remembered her harpoon tangling up in some sea weed as a teen and having to get her partner to release her.

Eirse found a good spot and settled in to wait, the cold, rough rock pressing against her shoulder. As her partner did the same at her back, she began to forget they were there. This was the part she didn't like… the waiting. They generally preferred to wait for large prey, especially when traveling to these depths. A large whale could support an entire community for ernos, and as long as they were conscientious about their hunting, it was a sustainable practice.

Various members of the community over the years had even come up with ways to encourage whales to come here and to other places nearby. There was an entire rift along the seafloor that they'd cultivated to provide their prey with everything they could possibly need. The floor was coated in a thick carpet of vegetation, which attracted smaller fish to flock there. This attracted the whales, and the deep rift made it harder for other predators to spot the whales from above.

Overall, it was a good practice, and it had been central to her people's survival for thousands of alos.

It was just boring as all get out.

One of the hardest things to learn as a hunter was how to keep focused when nothing was happening. While it was inevitable that a whale would come along eventually, it could be anywhere from a few diceros to several horos. There were regular pods that came through the area, but they could also be anywhere along the rift they'd cultivated. Hunters often picked a favorite spot and stayed put, maximizing their chances of catching a migrating whale.

Eirse yawned, small bubbles drifting out of her mouth. She looked around her, but could only see the barest traces of movement in the dark. And yet, she couldn't shake that feeling of foreboding from before. It was weird, like the feeling was coming from outside of herself somehow, like it didn't belong in this scene. And yet she couldn't shake it. A part of her was whispering that she should flee, but she couldn't. She felt like she was on rails, like what was about to happen was predestined.

And as quickly as those thoughts came to her, they left, drifting away on the currents. She saw a large body moving through the water off to her right and gripped her harpoon tighter. Preparing to strike, she leaned back one shoulder into her partner to let them know she'd seen something, and gripped the rope with her other hand.

She pushed away from the wall slightly, giving herself more room to throw. The creature continued moving farther and farther left in her field of vision. She pulled back her arm. She could feel her sail pulling taut as her arm reached full extension.

Eirse threw. The paler color of the shaft easily sailed through the water, connecting with her target's side moments later. She grabbed the rope with her now empty hand as her partner swam out, readying to unleash their own weapon at a closer, more lethal, distance.

That was when everything went wrong.

She watched in horror as her partner screamed, bubbles pouring out of their mouth as their prey suddenly changed direction.

No.

That's not a whale.

Eirse gripped her rope tighter, wrapping the length around her hands as she pushed off the seafloor, swimming away from her partner, hoping against hope the impossible would work. The sick feeling in her stomach told her exactly what was about to happen, but she refused to listen. She *knew* she couldn't swim well enough with her arms occupied holding the rope. She could either swim away and let her partner get eaten, or hold tight, her sails squashed against her sides, as she tried to keep the legendary Vrath from making a meal of both of them and ending this hunt before it had even got started.

This isn't happening.

Wake up. Just wake up.

But this wasn't a dream. This was real. It was happening. She pushed harder and harder with her feet, reaching the full extension of the rope, but instead of holding the monster back, *it* was pulling *her,* her body easily slipping through the water in the *wrong* direction.

"No!" she screamed, her words bubbling into the depths and rising uselessly to the surface.

The scent of blood in the water hit her, and she screamed again, panic hitting her hard. Were they okay? Were they dead?

Then the rope went slack. She tensed, not knowing what would come next.

Where is it?

Where's the threat?

Where's the Vrath?

She knew the dangers that lurked down here, was prepared for them, but nothing could have truly prepared her for an encounter with a Vrath. It was the only major predator that traveled this deep, and it often hunted the same whales they did, meaning that an encounter with one was always a possibility while hunting. Unfortunately, even an entire *team* of Tursiops couldn't go up against one and live.

The smell of blood swelled, and a part of her *knew* she couldn't save her partner. Her only option was escape now, and she wasn't sure she could make it. With the line slack, she had no way of knowing where the predator *was*. It could be anywhere within the range of the rope.

And definitely close enough to kill.

Her breathing became ragged as her mind ran in circles, trying to figure out a way to survive. Her muscles twitched, wanting to swim, wanting to hide, but she did nothing, paralyzed by fear, paralyzed by the unknown.

Suddenly, the currents shifted, and she jerked her attention to the left. Teeth opened wide in front of her, and she screamed. Dropping the rope from her nerveless fingers, she sped away, mindlessly praying for salvation. Pain lanced into her, and she could taste the blood in her mouth now. It hurt to use her left arm, the sail overwhelming her with piercing pain when she moved it.

Ignoring the pain, Eirse pushed herself as hard as she could. She needed to escape the beast's range. It was a deep sea predator. If she could just get closer to the surface, it would move on.

She swam upward, pleading for the beautiful teal and silver tones she'd seen earlier that erno or those rays of sunlight she'd been ogling, but she was so deep here. Around her, the sea was shades of black, giving nothing away. If she hadn't been born to this place, she wouldn't have even known which way was up, but her internal senses told her.

Another slice of searing pain hit her, this time streaking across her right sail and digging into her right calf. Panic hit her again, and she pushed herself harder. She was in constant pain now, her injuries begging her to stop, but the predator on her toes egged her onward.

She couldn't stop.

If she stopped, she was dead.

Eirse jerked awake, the adrenaline of the memory still rushing through her. The cool of the sea was replaced with the hot, dry air of the *Areon*. The smell of diluted blood was replaced with the slightly metallic tang of recycled air. The impenetrable darkness was replaced with the low light and metal surfaces of her bedroom.

"Another?" her roommate, Nella, said from across the room.

Eirse groaned and rolled over, not ready to deal with people just yet. That particular nightmare always lingered afterwards like a bad hangover.

Shuffling noises reached her as Nella moved about the room. "You should really talk to someone about those nightmares, Eirse. They're a bit of a problem."

"Suck my sails," Eirse said irritably as she sat up and slapped her feet against the cold floor.

"Fine," Nella said, raising her hands in defeat. "You want to wallow in your own self-pity, be my guest." She scoffed. "I'll just ask for a new roommate."

It was on the tip of her tongue to say something equally biting, but Nalla chose that moment to make her exit, the door slamming behind her. Eirse wanted to be mad at her, but she couldn't deny her roommate had a point. She'd woken Nalla from a deep sleep more times than she could count, and she couldn't really blame the other woman for wanting a decent night's rest.

Still, that didn't give her the right to tell her what to do.

Eirse stood, crossing to the built-in drawers on the back wall. Disengaging the lock, she pulled open the top drawer, diving her hands into the sea of unfolded uniforms, pulling out each needed item and throwing it at the bed. Once she had everything, she frowned down at the selection, not looking forward to wearing any of it. She was already overheating a little, and she was still naked from sleep.

Eirse's shoulders sagged, anticipating yet another erno sweating up her uniform. "I miss the sea." She reluctantly started getting dressed, pulling on each wrinkled garment with only the barest care for appearances. When she finished, she checked herself in the mirror above the drawers. For a moment, as she stared at her teal skin peeking out of her black uniform and her smooth purple hair falling behind her shoulders, she wondered what Taln would think. Would she be disgusted by the sloppy uniform? Or would she be captivated by her bright teal eyes, which she'd always felt were her best feature?

Eirse shook her head. "You have no idea what that woman wants."

She turned and headed toward the door, leaving her nightmares forgotten in her wake.

CHAPTER ONE

Taln woke before her alarm. She glanced over at the clock adhered to the wall by her pillow.

One dicero to go.

She shut off the alarm and rolled out of bed. Turning around, she fluffed her pillow and started making the bed, ensuring there were no wrinkles in the fabric.

Once satisfied, she walked to her drawers to start dressing. Each drawer was organized by type of garment and each item neatly folded. She dropped her pajamas into the dirty clothes receptacle and donned her uniform.

After adjusting the last item to her liking, she checked herself in the mirror, making sure nothing was out of place. Even her hair was just so, cropped tight to her head in a severe buzz cut. She smiled at her reflection and left the room.

"Captain," one of the crew said in passing as she exited her room.

Taln nodded at him and continued onward, focused on the next item on her mental To Do list. She usually had breakfast immediately after dressing. At the entrance to the dining hall, she stopped. Eirse was sitting at one of the tables. The other woman had been a problem for her ever since they'd recruited her away from the Diehli. Surg, owner of Inia Intergalactic (the company she worked for), had asked her to take Eirse under her wing and make sure she made the transition smoothly. There was only one problem.

She was hopelessly infatuated with the woman.

From the moment she'd first laid eyes on her, her libido had wanted nothing more than to get the other woman in her bed. Eirse was a Tursiops, an aquatic species she'd never encountered before, but that didn't stop her exotic teal skin, striking eyes, and amazingly powerful thighs from turning her on. Add in an attitude and confidence that just made her want to grab her and either strangle her or fuck her, and theirs was a relationship doomed to failure.

Because she couldn't. She just *couldn't*. Eirse was a subordinate, and while Inia Intergalactic didn't have any specific rules against fraternization, Taln did. Crossing those lines could make things complicated, and complicated could cost people their lives, especially in her line of work.

So, with a momentary regret, she straightened her shoulders, tilted her chin up just a little more, and crossed to the food storage and prep areas on the back wall. She tried not to let her gaze drift over Eirse's form, which filled out her uniform quite nicely.

Instead, she focused on breakfast, the din of the busy dining hall falling around her like a curtain. With practiced efficiency, she set about heating a cup of hal and hot cereal with berries. Meal in hand, she walked over to the only unoccupied table and sat down. She picked up her mug, letting it warm her hands as she blew on her hal, waiting for it to cool enough to drink. A sharp, energizing scent wafted up from its surface.

"Want company?" Eirse said, causing Taln to jump, almost spilling her morning pick-me-up.

Her nerves jangled a little as she recovered from being startled. Then, reasserting her usual calm demeanor, she turned to gaze at the other woman's beautiful, jewel-toned face. "Can I help you, Eirse?"

Eirse frowned, a certain calculating look in her eyes. She leaned forward, and Taln's gaze dropped to Eirse's cleavage, which was maximized by the sloppy way she'd done up her shirt today. As Taln continued to stare, she began to notice how Eirse's position enhanced the view even further. Eirse's hands were splayed on the table, her arms tightly framing her breasts, and she couldn't help approving of the pose.

Taln cleared her throat, forcing herself away from those unprofessional thoughts. Eirse was a subordinate. She couldn't put her in an awkward position by letting on how she felt. It would only cause problems.

So instead, she pointed a finger at Eirse's top and said, "Your shirt's come undone. You should fix that before you start your shift."

Eirse's face grew darker, her expression threatening violence as she pushed off the table. "And you should lighten up," she said before turning and storming out of the room, breathtaking in her anger.

Taln sighed and rested her chin on her unoccupied hand, the image of those powerful thighs haunting her long after Eirse was gone.

CHAPTER TWO

And that's *what I get for throwing myself at her...*

Eirse stormed off, very much wanting to hit something. Under ordinary circumstances, she would be heading to the *Areon's* security office where she worked when she wasn't in the field. Unfortunately, being cooped up in a small office with a locker full of weapons and nothing and no one to use them on was far from appealing right now. Just the thought of it made her skin crawl, so she sent a quick message to the lead security specialist, Xam, letting him know she would be practicing maneuvers in the gym this morning.

Thank the gods she had a job that allowed her the flexibility to vent her frustrations when she needed to.

She was about to open the steel door to the gym when her comm chimed.

"Excellent. I'll see you there," Xam's message read.

Oh, goodie. A sparring partner.

Which was really even better. Hitting up the equipment and running through maneuvers was good, but trying to beat the snot out of a coworker was better still. And Xam was no slouch. He was no Ateles, but he was all predator.

Eirse pushed the door open. The space was pretty big for the size of the ship, with a large sparring mat in the middle and equipment lining the mirrored walls. She crossed to the other side of the room and entered the changing area. To her right was a series of drawers with neatly organized shirts, pants, and shoes, all sorted by type and size. She grabbed what she needed and sat down on a bench to change, ignoring the small privacy rooms next to her.

She was just pulling on her pants when Xam stepped in, all thick green fur and teeth. Xam was a Lycaon, and they'd initially bonded over their mutual dislike of wearing shoes. The thick pads on Xam's feet made shoes sort of unnecessary and the loss of tactile stimuli counterproductive.

He also didn't like wearing clothes, another thing they'd bonded over, so when he stepped into the changing room, instead of reaching for the drawers, he just dropped the one article of clothing the company insisted on and barked, "You ready?"

Eirse smiled and nodded. "I am so gonna kick your ass."

He barked a laugh as he walked ahead of her to the sparring mat, his tail wagging happily behind him. "We'll just have to see about that." He stepped onto the mat, getting to the far end before turning around and settling into a fighter's stance, his sharp teeth alarmingly white in his furry green face. "Ready when you are, sweet cheeks."

Eirse stepped onto the mat. "Call me that again, and you won't live to see tomorrow."

He threw back his head and laughed again. "I'd love to see you try."

Eirse settled into her own fighter's stance, her webbed toes spreading wide on the spongy surface, arms and legs slightly bent and ready to respond to his slightest twitch. She watched his body language, which was admittedly difficult. Lycaons had thick fur covering their entire bodies, making it impossible to see the telltale signs of their muscles preparing to move. They also had a shorter range of facial expressions due to their elongated jaws. Often, the best places to watch a Lycaon were their pointed ears, which were extremely expressive, and their tails, which they used for balance. Their tails often moved right before they did.

A moment later, Eirse's hands were full of thick fur. With a careful twist, she spun around, locking Xam's arm behind his back. Still holding on, she grabbed his tail, yanking it hard, causing him to stumble then drop to the mat on his knees. She pushed, shoving his face to the floor, relishing the feel of having a man twice her size under her control.

She felt alive, a smile on her face as she panted lightly, her heartbeat singing in her ears. "Do you yield?"

Xam rolled over, taking her with him, but he didn't try to take advantage. "Of course, I yield. Good move."

Eirse let go, and he got to his feet, offering her a hand up. She didn't take it. After getting to her feet on her own, her smile stretched wider and she said, "Again?"

"Yeah." Behind him, his tail wagged happily.

This guy's insane.

After breakfast, Taln made her rounds. She didn't explicitly *need* to, but she liked checking in with her people. It was so much more efficient to have a dialog in person than through a comm. No waiting for responses and taking all erno to have a conversation that could have been resolved in less than three diceros.

Her first stop was the most important. Intelligence. She stepped into a relatively small room next to the control room. It was a simple space with three workstations, one on each wall, two of which were currently occupied. On the left, a young man, who didn't even look old enough to be working here, spun his chair around and saluted her, "Ma'am."

"At ease," she said in response, not even realizing she'd fallen into a ready stance. She relaxed, letting her hands drop to her sides.

The other person in the room held up a single finger before going back to finishing what she was doing. Moments passed with only the clicking of keys filling the silence. Then she spun her chair around as well and smiled, the fine lines around her eyes and mouth growing. "Captain," she said with a nod.

"Officer Sala. Any updates?"

"No, ma'am. I'm still waiting for a few of my contacts to get back to me. One seems really promising and one," she frowned, "seems like a bit of a long shot. The others I don't know yet. We'll see."

Taln nodded. She wasn't surprised. A few morgos back, Surg had called her into his office and offered her a role in taking down the Diehli, a company that had been a thorn in their side for alos. They were a nasty piece of work, a company that sold dangerous tech to even more dangerous people and wasn't opposed to hiring mercenaries to get what they wanted, even when it didn't belong to them. Hael, *especially* when it didn't belong to them. They'd been involved in everything from piracy to government conspiracies.

She'd happily agreed to help.

But deciding to take down the Diehli was one thing. Actually doing it was something else entirely. Surg had teams all over Inia Intergalactic working on the project, including their very own in-house privateer, Cassandra Allen. She could only imagine what the shape-shifting pirate was currently up to, but at the moment, it didn't matter.

What mattered was completing her own small part in this war. That included assigning Officer Sala to find her targets. They'd already taken down several valuable installations. A manufacturing plant. A research facility. A cargo ship filled with illicit merchandise. Each time was exhilarating, but she knew it wasn't the end. She wasn't sure what that end would look like for the Diehli, but if she could help make it happen, that was enough for her.

"Thank you, Officer Sala, for all your hard work. If you need anything, just let me know."

"Always, Captain," Sala said with a respectful nod.

"I'll leave you to it then."

Eirse stepped into the Security Office, her previous annoyance with Taln burned off by a long session of beating the crap out of Xam.

"Who won?" someone asked, not even turning away from their computer screen.

"Who do you think?" she snapped, feeling annoyed all over again. When had Xam *ever* won a sparring match against her? Sometimes, she wondered if the big floof *liked* getting his ass kicked by a girl.

She very much suspected the answer was yes, yes, he did.

She crossed the room, ignoring the rest of the poor souls occupying it. While the Security Office was larger than most of the other rooms in the ship, it was still cramped for a team their size. And that was *before* Xam walked through the door.

He stepped through smelling like damp fur, and she couldn't help wondering if Lycaons sweated. She didn't, but she knew plenty of species that did, including Taln, who looked absolutely fantastic with a sheen of sweat making her muscles glisten. It was enough to make even the most kick-ass female swoon. She held in a sigh. There was no way in the Nine Depths she was letting a girly sigh slip from her lips in *this* crowd.

Eirse dropped into a seat at the back of the room and pulled up security feeds as the rest of the team started razzing Xam for getting his butt kicked again. She tuned it out, focusing instead on making sure the ship was safe and secure. It was by far the most boring part of working for Inia Intergalactic. She almost *missed* being trapped in that stupid space station back at Diehli. At least then, she'd had the option of making rounds, walking about and pretending to be useful. But there was really next to nothing for her to do on this ship.

When they had a mission, it was different. She could breach other ships or go planetside. She could fire guns, fight, and take out bad guys. It was rewarding and exciting, but the times in between could be absolutely brutal for such a normally active person.

So after she'd finished checking all the external sensors manually, a crucial part of combating modern stealth technology, she switched to the cameras monitoring the inside of the ship. It wasn't necessary, but at least it gave her something to do.

And when she spotted Taln walking down the hall, she zoomed in.

That is one fine ass.

Eirse just sat there for a moment, the computer's cursor resting over Taln's right butt cheek, and sighed, unable to keep it in any longer.

"What's this?" Xam said, his furry bulk surrounding her from behind.

"Nothing." Thankfully, her voice didn't squeak in her panic like it used to. It was bad enough people tended to say her voice sounded like a song or tinkling bells, which usually resulted in a healthy bout of violence, but having them find out she was crushing on the captain? That would be devastating. She would never hear the end of it.

"That doesn't look like nothing," Xam continued, poking a finger at the screen as Taln walked down the hallway, her ass swaying back and forth in a hypnotic rhythm. "Looks like you're stalking the cap."

Eirse surged from her seat in one motion, knocking Xam backward. "I am not!" she shouted, but her soft voice cut some of the bark from the words, undermining her yet again.

Xam smirked, the expression barely registering beneath the heavy layer of fur. He turned his head back toward the rest of the team, who had all stood up themselves to see what the fuss was about. "I think something hit a nerve." He turned back to her. "Does someone have the hots for the captain?"

"No," she said, but her cheeks darkened anyway, belying her statement. "Of course not."

"Now, Eirse," one of her coworkers said, dropping a heavy arm on her shoulder from behind. "There's nothing wrong with a little harmless infatuation."

"Besides," a deep voice said from the back of the room, "that woman needs a fuck something serious."

"Yeah, then she might ease up a little."

"You're…" Eirse looked around the room, her brain slow to process what she was hearing. "You're okay with this?"

"Sure," Xam said. "Eirse, come on. You've been drooling all over the captain from the moment you came on board."

"You knew," she said incredulously, looking around and expecting one of the beefy security personnel surrounding her to laugh and admit they were pulling a prank on her.

"Well, sure. We've actually been putting bets on who was going to make the first move and when. We keep doubling up the bet every time nobody wins."

Someone in the crowd snorted. "Yeah, at this point, we need to move this along or all of us are gonna go broke."

Eirse laughed. At first, it was just a "ha" that popped from her throat, a little expression of surprise, really. Then she did it again, three this time. Then she couldn't stop. She laughed until there were tears in her eyes. She laughed until her jaw and sides hurt. She laughed until she could barely breathe.

When she finally straightened, taking a few unsteady breaths, everyone was looking at her funny, like they were afraid she'd snapped. "I'm okay, guys." She smiled weakly, feeling awkward now that the hysterical laughing fit had ended. She couldn't believe they'd known all along. How had she missed them placing bets on her love life? And yet it was sort of sweet. They'd been rooting for her. They hadn't been betting on *if* she would get the girl, but when.

For a brief, beautiful moment, it made the impossible seem within reach. What if she *could* have Taln? What if Taln liked her back?

She smiled and couldn't help hoping.

Taln stepped into her office feeling listless. She hated this. She hated feeling like this. It wasn't like her, at least not the person everyone knew. Everyone knew she could handle a great deal of things. In fact, she'd been praised for her ability to stay calm under fire. Her demeanor had been part of the reason she'd rapidly risen through the ranks to the role of captain.

But when things were quiet, that facade fell apart.

Her fists clenched at her sides as she crossed the small room to her desk. But when she reached it, she hesitated, not wanting to sit down. She looked around the room, realizing just how empty it was. Everything was put away, nothing on the walls, nothing on the desk. Everything was factory default, nothing modified, nothing custom. There was nothing in this room that spoke of her personality. If she died today, there was nothing her successor would have to remove.

That thought sent a chill through her. This job had been the best thing to happen to her. Before Surg had taken a chance on her, she'd had nothing. She'd been an orphan, a child abandoned on an alien world. She'd been cared for and provided for growing up, but she'd discovered pretty quickly that employers on that planet always hired natives. Taln had put herself out there in a blur of interviews, but employer after employer had chosen someone else.

Always. Someone. Else.

Surg had been the first person to give her a chance. He'd been the first to look beyond her physical differences. He'd looked past the fact that her ears were the wrong shape and her skin tone was just slightly different from everyone else's. She'd been desperate for a shot, and he'd given it to her. She'd always been grateful for that.

But in moments like these, when she wasn't busy and there was nothing to distract her, she started to feel like that small orphan once more, abandoned in the streets of a planet that clearly wasn't home, surrounded by people who looked nothing like her. Anxiety started to spike in her blood, making her tense, making her shake.

She leaned against the cold metal wall, letting the sensation seep into her, hoping it would make some sort of difference. "I am accomplished. I am good at what I do. I am not a child anymore." *I am safe.* The last part she couldn't even bring herself to say aloud. She had a good job, had put away plenty of money for emergencies. If she needed to, she could quit tomorrow, relocate somewhere else, find another position, and probably still have money left over, but sometimes she still didn't feel secure. Sometimes, she just couldn't make herself feel stable no matter how much she controlled her environment. No amount of hierarchy, rules and regulations, or likely compulsively perfectionist behavior helped in those instances.

Sometimes, she just couldn't escape her past, no matter how hard she tried.

Then her comm sounded, dragging her out of her mood. She stood up straight and tall, readjusted her shirt, and took a deep, steadying breath before walking to her desk and tapping the display to initiate the video call. "Yes, Officer Sala?"

"Good news. We've got something."

Thank the gods.

CHAPTER THREE

I get to see her.

That was the first thought that popped into Eirse's head when she received the notification about a briefing later that erno, followed immediately by *I'm hopeless.*

It felt good, though, having her coworkers, her team, on her side. They knew how she felt about Taln and wanted to help. She'd spent most of the rest of the erno with them offering aid in various ways. Just thinking about it made her smile, remembering the way they'd interspersed their assistance with little nudges encouraging her to get down to business on set timeframes.

Nobody had forgotten the bet.

When she sat down at the *Areon's* sole conference table later that erno, she was practically bubbling with anticipation, though she felt she did a pretty good job hiding it. The rest of the room was paying her no mind as she slouched in her chair, giving off an apathetic air that practically everyone expected from her at this point. All things considered, it was a fairly small room, and at times, it could get quite crowded. Today wasn't too bad, with only a couple members of her team standing against the wall. The table and its chairs took up most of the space. Each person around it served as contrast to her, sitting upright and wearing their clothes as neat as a military uniform. It left her the odd man out.

Like always.

She'd had a hard time adapting to working at Inia at first, dismissing offers of friendship and glaring or snarling at people when they tried to be nice to her. She was used to the cutthroat environment at Diehli, where an offered hand, more often than not, was attached to a conniving mind waiting to stab you in the back. It took a while to trust. It was going to take even longer to break those initial impressions of her she'd made here.

Though the situation with the security team was a good start. Eirse hadn't realized how they saw her until today. She knew Xam liked getting his ass handed to him on a regular basis, which she was happy to oblige, but that was about it. She wasn't even friends with Xam. He was just a convenient sparring partner when she wanted to let off some steam.

But now she felt like maybe something more was brewing, like maybe for the first time in alos, she could actually have friends. Eirse couldn't even remember what that was like anymore. She'd spent so much time punishing herself for the accident that took her sails. She'd believed she didn't deserve better than the Diehli. In her mind, she'd belonged there. She'd felt she was, in her own way, just as bad as them.

And yet she'd been just as isolated at Diehli as she was now. She realized she'd fallen into a habit of self-isolation that reinforced itself again and again, preventing herself from ever having friends, from ever being loved.

But she didn't have to do that anymore. No one here cared about what happened back on her homeworld. Most of them probably didn't even realize she was disabled. And unless she was faced with swimming in a body of water, no one ever needed to learn the difference. She could start fresh here, make a new life for herself. It wouldn't be the life she'd expected to live back home, but that didn't mean it couldn't be a good one. She could have friends and love. She could be happy.

Then, as if to put an exclamation point on her thoughts, Taln walked into the room, looking as poised, tall, and perfectly put together as always. A small smile tipped Eirse's lips upward.

And it all starts with her.

Taln stepped into the conference room, observing the haphazard assortment of personnel assembled around the table. Though everyone was in uniform, that was where their uniformity ended. Different species, different genders and sexes, different career paths, different attitudes. A couple of her security officers were standing at the back of the room, leaning against the wall with their arms crossed. Everyone else was seated, though in one instance, "seated" was a bit of a stretch.

Her gaze settled on Eirse, who was currently lounging in a sprawl that made it look like she was on vacation or something. Taln didn't say anything, even though she probably would have given any other member of her crew an earful.

She clasped her hands behind her back, straightening her spine. "All right, let's get started, everyone. Sala?"

"Yes, Captain." The older woman shifted in her seat before leaning over and activating the display built into the table.

Shortly after, the walls lit up, mirroring the table's screen. "Earlier today, I received intelligence about this planet. It has no name that we know of, but we have reason to believe there is a Diehli installation on its surface. I received the following scans from my source." The screen changed, showing what looked like a ship-bound scan for tech. A small region, barely larger than a finger, even on the wall displays, flared bright red on the otherwise dim overlay of the planet. "My sources tell me there was a significant movement of building supplies and laboratory equipment to this sector of space about three alos ago, which is unusual since it's nowhere near any shipping lanes or inhabited planets. This is the only planet I've been able to find that could have received those shipments. I traced the purchase orders for those shipments back to a holding company used by the Diehli."

"Do we know what they're doing there?"

Officer Sala shook her head. "Unfortunately, no. What I have been able to ascertain is that the Diehli have put a lot of money into this sector. It's safe to say, this *means* something to them."

"And that means it means something to us," Taln interjected. "The current strategy is to take a small team planetside, determine the nature and threat level of the facility, then regroup. At the moment, we know *nothing* about what they're working on, but we do know what equipment they have. Because of that," she motioned at Officer Sala, who changed the view to a clearer map image of the surface, with dots highlighting points of interest, "we'll be keeping the *Areon* on the other side of the planet at all times to prevent it from being detected by ground systems.

"Once in geostationary orbit, we'll send down a shuttle with myself and Officer Eirse aboard, landing here." Taln indicated a spot on the map. "Then we'll travel on foot to the facility here and gather intel. Once we've gathered sufficient information, we'll return to the shuttle and then back to the ship. I'll be making judgment calls on the ground as to how far we should go with our information gathering."

Xam, her lead security specialist, pushed off the wall and stepped up to the table. "But wouldn't it be better to send a larger team, even if they stay at the shuttle? Backup in case something happens? With the current plan, you won't be able to send transmissions to the *Areon* if you need assistance."

Taln nodded. "That's correct. Based on what we know of the shipments sent to this sector of space, that facility has the capacity to intercept transmissions. Any comms coming from or going to that side of the planet can be intercepted, and we should assume they *will* be. We can't risk anything but comm silence until we know more about the situation."

"And what if something goes wrong?"

Taln thought about it. How long would it take for them to get in and out? "Give 15 horos. If we haven't reinitiated contact by then, send the second shuttle with the remainder of the security team."

"Yes, ma'am." Xam backed up, leaning against the wall once more.

Taln turned to the navigator. "How long until we reach our destination?"

A man close to the head of the table leaned over, tapping the display and doing some quick calculations, then looked up again. "Should be about thirty four horos."

"All right. Everyone dismissed. Be ready in thirty four horos."

Eirse was quiet as she left the conference room, her stomach fluttering with nerves or excitement or both. She wasn't quite sure.

This felt like kismet, like the forces of the universe were aligning all at the same time, ensuring she would have her perfect shot at happiness. First she'd gotten the support of her team, then she'd found out she was going on a mission *alone* with her crush? Could this *get* any more perfect?

Not bloody likely.

And yet… what was she going to do? How was she going to get Taln to see how she felt about her? What if Taln didn't return her feelings? For all she knew, the other woman strictly liked men. That was common, wasn't it? Not super common, but it happened a good deal of the time. There were plenty of people who were not interested in same-gender relationships. It was a thing.

As she stepped back into the security office, her stomach soured as worry and anxiety ate away at her.

"You look like you're about to throw up."

"Shut up," she said, not even stopping to check who'd spoken before dropping into her seat and staring blankly at the dark screen before her.

Maybe this is a bad idea.

She found herself idly rubbing the scar that peeked out of her shirt sleeve. The thick line of rough dark skin ran all the way up the inside of her arm and down her flank on each side, a constant reminder of what she'd been through. She closed her eyes and took a deep breath, gripping her wrist to stop herself from continuing the nervous tick.

Then a new, more alarming thought occurred to her. What if her plan put them in danger? They were going into an uncertain, potentially dangerous situation. How stupid would it be to split their focus with her seduction routine? What if that got Taln hurt or even killed?

I couldn't live with myself.

"You trying to back out?" Xam asked, leaning a hip against the console next to her.

"What?" she said, looking up… and up, her seated position putting her at a severe disadvantage.

"You were shaking your head and muttering to yourself."

"I don't mutter."

He snorted. "Keep telling yourself that."

She opened her mouth to snap some snide reply back at him, but her mind went blank.

"So, what's the problem?"

She started rubbing her scar again. "I was thinking about seducing Taln during the mission, but I think it might be a bad idea."

"Well," he said, slouching down to put himself closer to eye level with her. It didn't help. "I think that's going to very much depend on what the situation is like down there. Certainly, I wouldn't suggest trying anything if the two of you need to be on high alert. To the Depths with the bet if the two of you aren't safe."

Eirse smiled at his use of a Tursiops curse.

"That being said, if it does seem safe, if the two of you can drop your guard for a spell, it's probably a perfect opportunity. The two of you will be alone, nice romantic setting…"

"Romantic setting? We know nothing about the ecosystem. It could be swamplands."

He shrugged. "It's romantic to some people."

She shook her head, but then smiled. "Thanks, Xam. I think I needed that."

"Anytime, killer."

Maybe that was a bad idea.

Taln had kept her composure until she reached her room, letting the door slip closed behind her before she let the mask drop. Instantly, it felt like a massive weight had fallen off of her. And yet she was still tense, still agitated. She started pacing across the small room, wall to bed and back again.

Did I rush this?

She'd created plenty of mission plans with less time. In fact, she'd spent all afternoon working out the details from what little information she had. On paper, it had all seemed solid enough.

And yet now she was second guessing herself. Something felt wrong, and it left her feeling stressed, running through the mission over and over again in her head, searching for a flaw, searching for the mistake she'd made.

The plan seemed simple enough. Approach the facility with a small crew, investigate without being detected, and then get out. Easy.

When she'd been formulating the plan, Eirse had seemed the perfect option. They needed a small team. They needed to get out quickly and quietly, and *no one* was as good at quick and quiet as Eirse. She'd settled on a two-person team because she was worried about being detected. The more people she sent down to the surface, the greater the probability of being spotted. A two-man crew could get in and out far better than half a dozen.

And yet with all that in mind, she still couldn't escape the nagging worry that Eirse was the wrong choice for the mission.

She stopped her pacing and sat down on the edge of her bed. What if Eirse proved to be a distraction? She couldn't deny she found the woman distracting. She was drawn to watching her anytime they were in the same room together.

And yet they'd performed well enough on missions together in the past. On Wesa, they'd fought back to back without fail, her unhealthy fixation on her subordinate not getting in the way of protecting the small village of Valana. They'd walked away from that conflict unscathed, and that wasn't the first time they'd fought side by side on missions.

Or the last.

So why was she questioning her own judgment? She'd been a captain for alos. She was well trusted by the leaders of Inia Intergalactic. What was she so concerned about? Why did this mission leave her feeling so uneasy?

Was it the unknown?

And yet she'd gone into plenty of missions with less than ideal quantities of intelligence. That was nothing new. She could happily go into a mission with almost no information so long as she was sufficiently prepared.

Was it a lack of preparation?

Except, they had ernos until the mission start. She could easily spend every moment between now and then running through every possible scenario and planning for every eventuality.

Which brought her right back to Eirse. She realized this would be the first time she'd been alone on a mission with Eirse. In the past, they'd either been a part of a larger team or there had been allies around them. They'd never been alone on a mission before.

But why would that make any difference? Eirse was capable and enthusiastic, a valuable asset on any mission. But she was also irreverent, and maybe that was part of the reason she was hesitating. Eirse had little respect for authority, willfully bucked convention whenever she felt like it, and voiced her opinion even when it would have been far smarter not to. She was a wild card even under the best of circumstances, and yet she was bringing her on a mission where predictability might mean the difference between life and death.

And what about her past? She was bringing her alone on a mission against the Diehli, the very company they'd recruited her from. Taln didn't honestly believe Eirse would want to return to Diehli, but you never knew with people. Diehli wasn't exactly known for hiring the most loyal or reliable people. Eirse seemed different, but appearances could be deceiving.

Was she really ready to put Eirse's loyalty to the test?

CHAPTER FOUR

he next couple ernos went by quickly for Eirse. She sparred with Xam, checked and rechecked her equipment, and schemed with her coworkers, planning various ways she could seduce their boss.

Most of the scheming seemed to be in jest, though, much to her disappointment. Everyone seemed to want to calm her nerves more than give her good ideas. She still had to hold in a chuckle every time the suggestion she'd received from one coworker of just "showing her what she was missing" surfaced in her brain. Apparently, for his species, stripping and presenting your junk to a potential partner was perfectly normal.

While nudity wasn't exactly something she had a problem with, she just couldn't see herself stripping in front of Taln, apropos of nothing. Even the idea of it had her anxiety spiking.

Then, sharp as a well-hewn blade, the intercom interrupted her musings. "We are currently approaching the planet. We should be in geostationary orbit within the next five diceros. Everyone, please report to your relevant stations."

Eirse stood up. "Well, that's my cue."

"You ready?"

She turned to her coworkers. Each of them had stupid grins on their faces. She shook her finger at them. "You all need to get your own bloody sex lives. You're entirely too invested in mine."

A laugh came from the back of the room. "Hey. We take our bets seriously around here."

She snorted and walked away. "Apparently."

Eirse didn't bother heading back to her bunk. She had already packed what she would need and had loaded it up on the shuttle a couple horos ago. The walk to the shuttle bay was quick, interspersed with occasional absentminded greetings from people returning to their stations. In comparison to previous missions, there were noticeably fewer people in the hallways, giving the impression that nothing especially important was happening, but that was an illusion brought on by the peculiar nature of the mission. Unlike most missions, once they took off, there was nothing anyone on the ship could do to help.

Even so, the shuttle bay crew still needed to do final prep and checks of the shuttle, and security personnel would still need to be at their stations in case the shuttle was spotted by the Diehli before it left comms range. If things went wrong early on, the *Areon* would come in guns blazing, backing up their shuttle until it could return to the ship.

When she walked into the shuttle bay, she smiled. It was a hive of activity this soon before a launch. People in coveralls barked out commands and status updates while swarming over practically every surface of the shuttle. The shuttle itself was fairly small, designed for at most six people (if you didn't mind practically sitting on someone's lap). They had a second, larger one on the other side of the bay, but it wouldn't be necessary for this mission. In fact, the much smaller shuttle was ideal for sneaking in and out undetected. It had modern stealth technology, including a little something they'd stolen from the Diehli not that long ago, and it was small enough to fall below the lower limit of detection of the types of systems installed in larger ships, stations, and facilities.

"How we doing, folks?" she asked as she crossed the room.

Someone who seemed to be in charge stepped back and rubbed his hands on a filthy rag. "Almost done. We're just running final checks now. You should be ready to go by the time we reach geostationary orbit."

"Excellent. Good job."

He nodded, then went back to calling out orders to his crew.

Eirse walked around the back of the shuttle, stepping in to do a final check on her gear. Since they would likely spend less than an erno on the planet and would spend most of their time away from the shuttle, she'd settled for light and portable. Her weapons were all either silent by nature (knives and staves) or were special models designed for stealth. She'd chosen lighter weight guns, a moderate amount of ammunition, and a retractable staff, along with a few throwing knives to fill out her arsenal. Her pack contained food, water, filtration equipment, some very basic camping gear, a first aid kit, and little else. It weighed less than some of the guns she'd used in the past.

"Eirse!"

She spun around at hearing Taln's voice. "Yeah, Captain?"

"I just got the final report about the ecosystem we'll be landing in." Taln was walking across the bay wearing camo gear, an identical material shoved under her arm. "Here," she said as she reached the end of the shuttle's ramp.

Eirse took the stack of clothing, the green, gray, and black material coarse against her fingers and palms. The uniform easily went on over her black t-shirt and base-layer tights. The fit was baggy, making it easy to move in and would be quite breathable should they end up somewhere humid, not that she had a problem with humidity. She tended to prefer it. It was probably one of the few times her skin didn't feel just a little itchy from dryness.

"All right, you're all clear," the crew chief said from somewhere outside the shuttle.

Taln nodded. "You good, Eirse?"

"I am if you are."

Taln nodded and walked past her, settling into one of the seats at the front of the shuttle. Eirse followed suit, dropping into the seat next to her and clipping the harness in place.

Taln opened comms. "We are good to go. Clear the bay."

Through the main screen, Eirse watched as people hustled out of sight.

"The bay is clear. Opening bay doors," a voice said over comms.

Eirse leaned back, a small smile touching her lips. She'd always preferred being on missions. Being stuck on a ship or space station was boring, not to mention those spaces were generally optimized for beings very different from her own. And while she could spar all she wanted with Xam, nothing was quite like being in the thick of it. Not knowing if you were safe or not. Feeling that surge of excitement when you heard a noise, and you weren't sure if it was a threat or not. There was really nothing like it.

The engines kicked on, a surprisingly gentle hum that gradually increased in volume. Life Support systems turned on next, a rush of air pouring into the small cabin.

"Ready to depart," Taln said as the bay doors started rolling open.

It probably only took moments, but it felt like diceros passed as they waited for the opening to grow large enough for their shuttle to pass through.

"Departing now," Taln said as her hands moved to the controls. The shuttle lifted gently off the floor and eased forward, slipping through the growing gap.

There was silence in the shuttle as they cleared the door and started their descent to the planet's surface. It was possibly the perfect time to start her campaign to win Taln, but her mind suddenly blanked, all the strategies she'd made in the last few ernos just gone. She looked over at Taln, who looked austere as she smoothly piloted the shuttle, as oblivious as always to Eirse's interest.

Out of her peripheral vision, her view of the mostly green planet was blotted out by a moon for a few moments, like a shadow crossing over the sun. She turned back to the viewscreen. "Is that safe?" she asked, noticing how close the satellite was to their ship.

"Oh, yes. The pilot took the moon's orbital path into consideration."

Eirse nodded. She suddenly realized she knew absolutely nothing about piloting or navigation. Even this shuttle, as simple as it probably was, was a complete mystery to her. She very much doubted she could fly it in an emergency. And what if something happened to Taln? What if she couldn't fly the shuttle back to the ship? Eirse would be just as likely to kill them both as bring the shuttle back safely. And they were on comm silence until the mission was over, so they couldn't even call for help. Was she really the best person for this mission? Maybe Taln should have picked someone else?

Thank the gods they had a failsafe. Fifteen horos and if things went wrong, a rescue team would come get them. At worst, she would have to hold out until help could arrive. Fifteen horos was nothing.

The pull on the shuttle changed as they entered the atmosphere, and a red sheen tinted the viewscreen. Eirse leaned back in her seat, preparing for the increasing force of reentry. It wouldn't be long now until they reached their landing point.

Diceros ticked by as she was pushed back into her seat more and more. She closed her eyes, not liking how the world seemed to whiz by around them in a disorienting way. Eirse was a security person, a fighter. She was best with solid ground beneath her feet. She'd never been in the front seat when taking off or landing before, and she suddenly wished she wasn't now. Her stomach roiled alarmingly as she prayed to the gods for this to be over soon, but she feared she would sooner reach the Nine Depths than safely walk on solid earth once more.

Time dragged on, her discomfort making it feel like an eternity. She wanted to go back and just forget about the mission and her plans for Taln. Her stomach felt like it was leaping into her throat, threatening a revolt.

When will this end?

"You can open your eyes now," Taln said beside her, a hint of amusement in her voice.

Eirse realized she was digging gouges into the armrests with her nails, and her back was pressed so firmly into the cushioning that she hadn't even realized when they'd stopped. She peeked a single eye open, spotting stationary greenery before her.

"We've landed," Taln said as she leaned over Eirse, a smirk on her face.

"Oh, shut up," Eirse snapped defensively, pushing Taln aside and rushing to get out of her seat. Her cheeks heated alarmingly in her embarrassment, and she covered it up by turning her back on Taln to retrieve her gear. She focused for several diceros on loading her weapons into harnesses, checking safeties, and adjusting the straps on her pack. When she turned around again, her cheeks had cooled to normal levels.

Taln was already geared up, her elegant hands on her straps as she rolled her shoulders to get the pack's weight just right. "We'll travel for about ten diceros, then readjust our packs. Check your wrist comm and set up your HUD. You should have all the mission data on it."

Eirse pulled her HUD out of her pack. This HUD was one of the less intrusive models, just an ear piece with a display that covered one eye. She situated it on her right ear and powered it on. A boot sequence flickered over the display before it returned to a blank screen, the default. Then she shifted her attention to her wrist comm, where she selected "Mission" from the menu screen. It gave multiple options, and she scrolled to "Map Overlay." A moment later, the HUD lit up with a red line indicating their planned path to the facility discovered by Officer Sala. "Ready when you are."

Taln nodded and moved to the back of the shuttle, pressing a button to open the rear door. As the door opened, the natural scent of the planet filled the room and Eirse breathed deep, a small smile spreading across her face. Great Depths, it was always good to smell something other than recirculated air and sweaty bodies.

"Yeah, that's a good feeling, isn't it?" Taln said, smiling next to her.

Eirse looked over at her and felt at peace. She wanted to reach out to Taln and take her hand. It felt like a couples moment. But they weren't a couple, and she tried hard to keep the smile on her face as that reality took the water out of her sails. "Shall we?" she said, wondering if Taln could hear the strain in her voice.

"Yes, best get started."

Taln stepped onto the ramp, and in a bittersweet moment, Eirse admired her, thinking she looked like a conquering hero as she stomped down to the damp earth awaiting them.

Eirse was acting weird.

After their first break, where they'd adjusted their packs, Taln had taken to staying in the lead, not knowing what to do with her companion's odd mood. She could tell something was bothering the other woman, but had no idea what.

And a part of her was concerned it would affect the mission. Bad things could happen when people were distracted or not in the right headspace. And Eirse was usually solid as a rock. In spite of her history and personality, she was pretty dependable, often eager to get into dangerous situations, even against the Diehli, but now she seemed distracted and deep in her own thoughts.

She slowed down, letting Eirse catch up with her. According to her HUD, they weren't far from the facility now, and if they needed to hash something out, it would be better to do it now when they weren't within earshot of the facility. "What's up?"

Eirse looked over at her, looking perturbed. "Nothing, Captain."

"Now, you and I *both* know that's not true. Something's clearly bothering you. So, what is it?"

Eirse shook her head. "Nothing you need to be concerned with, ma'am."

Taln paused. Eirse wasn't usually that formal with her. Or anyone, really. Something was clearly wrong. She stepped in front of Eirse, forcing her to stop. "I need you focused, Eirse. Your distraction could get us both killed."

Eirse stopped, seeming surprised by Taln's statement. "I'm not distracted, Captain."

"Try spitting those lies at someone who'll believe them," she snapped, getting irritated with her subordinate. Usually, she had a lot of patience with Eirse, probably because she found her so bloody attractive. It took everything she had to keep things professional, so being stern with her was usually out of the question, but she couldn't afford leniency right now. They were on a mission, a mission that had them going deep into the unknown, exploring an enemy facility they knew nothing about. They needed to be sharp. They needed to be ready for any eventuality. They couldn't afford a single mistake.

Eirse looked away and finally admitted, "I have a lot on my mind."

Taln leaned in. "Well, clear it. We need to focus, okay? We'll be back to the ship in a matter of horos. You can ruminate on those things to your heart's content once we get back. If you need it, I'll even give you some time off."

Eirse closed her eyes and nodded.

"Good. Now, let's move."

They continued onward, and this time, she could feel the difference in Eirse. She still wasn't her normal self, but at least she seemed more focused, more aware. She had a hand resting on a knife strapped to her chest, her head swiveling slightly to take in their surroundings. Her footsteps were more sure as well, each footfall made with precision.

Taln relaxed a little, letting her attention move back to the world around them. They were surrounded by trees and low-lying brush, all with green vegetation of varying shades clinging to their branches. The air was still, redolent with a sort of earthy decay and thick with humidity. It felt alive, and the calls of insects and native animal species concurred with that. In that moment, it was hard to imagine that, in a matter of diceros, they would reach an advanced research laboratory built by their enemy.

Eirse tapped Taln's shoulder, drawing her out of a reverie she'd scolded her subordinate for only moments before. She focused on the direction Eirse was pointing, spotting a glint of silver among the trees. She nodded and pulled a gun from one of her holsters, lifting it to shoulder height as she advanced. It was too soon to have reached the facility, leaving her both curious and annoyed at the mystery of its presence. Her HUD still indicated they had farther to go, and off to the right, not in this direction.

They moved silently through the underbrush, dropping to a crouch when they reached the edge of a clearing, where a shuttle waited, looking dilapidated and abandoned. She looked over at Eirse, feeling confused, then tapped on her wrist comm, running a scan for active tech and body heat. She came up with nothing, not even so much as a security camera or audio recording device. With a hand gesture, they both stood and left cover, slowly approaching the ship.

As they grew closer, it looked in worse shape than they'd originally thought. Shadows from the trees overhead had masked some of the damage, making it look better than it really was. The shuttle's surface was streaked with dirt, probably from repeated rainstorms, and the landing gear was buried in hardened mud. It was not currently under power, and as they approached the rear, there was visible damage to the engines, like something or someone had attacked it again and again and again. It was so torn up, she couldn't tell what had done the damage.

But the rear door was probably the worst. As they stopped at the back of the shuttle, Eirse muttered, "Great Depths," under her breath, and Taln couldn't disagree. She was equally shocked. She'd never seen this type of damage in her life. The upper left corner of the door looked like it had been peeled back, like a field ration kit opened by an especially impatient soldier.

"What could do that?" she wondered aloud, not expecting an answer. Maybe not wanting one.

Suddenly, she had a very bad feeling about this mission.

CHAPTER FIVE

y the time they left the disabled shuttle behind, Eirse was no longer distracted. If anything, she was the opposite of distracted. She was on edge and waiting for an attack she suspected was right around the corner. When they'd departed on this mission, the last thing she'd expected was *that*.

What in the Nine Depths happened here?

Eirse sheathed her knife, switching to a gun. She slipped back into the trees, taking the lead this time. A red line continued to streak across her HUD like an ominous portent, leading them to their doom.

Behind her, Taln was silent, the only sounds coming from native wildlife around them. She stepped carefully, but still managed to cross the forest with speed. Then Eirse caught a whiff of brackish water, and a wave of homesickness hit her without warning. She stumbled and stared off to her right.

Between the trees, she could just barely spot the water beyond. It seemed to have a silvery shimmer in the late afternoon sunlight, surprising her even more. She'd been expecting something green, dark, or brown. She closed her eyes, remembering the silver sheen to the water back home, interrupted only by waves and ripples on the surface. The water had reflected the nearly constant cloud cover her homeworld was known for, giving it a beautiful shimmer like finely crafted metals.

Taln bumped her shoulder, and she shook herself and continued walking, only then realizing she'd been absently rubbing the scar on one of her forearms. She dropped her hands to her sides, annoyed with her stupid reverie.

Move on.

You can't go back home.

It wouldn't have mattered anyway. She'd left for a reason. And not just because she'd felt at fault for her hunting partner's death.

No, she'd left because she was worthless in the water now. Without sails, she couldn't survive on her homeworld anymore. She'd stayed for a spell after the tragedy, first in the water with the rest of her people, then on the land, but she'd been kidding herself.

Where before she'd been able to provide food for her people, suddenly she could barely swim. She'd been prone to infections, constantly sick, constantly needing someone else to care for her.

Eventually, she'd given up. She couldn't handle being a burden. She couldn't handle the looks people gave her or the way swimming suddenly felt like practically moving backwards rather than gliding through the water.

Eirse had left, hoping to find peace with her lot in life, but she'd never been able to achieve it. She'd taken the job with the Diehli for that very reason, she suspected. Diehli was the worst type of business, one that saw nothing as sacred and worked with the most disreputable clients in the universe. At the time, she'd felt like she deserved no better. And she'd continued to think so for alos.

Until Taln.

Until Taln and her crew had invaded Diehli headquarters to rescue someone.

Eirse smirked.

She herself had been tasked with finding the wayward inventor and had bumped into Taln's team in the process. She'd maybe expected a bullet in the head, not a job offer.

That moment changed her life. She actually felt like she had a chance at happiness now. Even if every advance she made on Taln failed, even if she never found love, she could be happy here. She had a fulfilling job, maybe even friends, and she had actually started the process of forgiving herself. Being with Taln would be a gift, but she couldn't deny she'd come a long way already.

Taln's arm came up beside her from behind, motioning toward something ahead of them.

Eirse stopped and focused in the direction she'd pointed, immediately spotting what Taln had seen. Sharp lines peeked through the leaves, likely the edges of the building. It was made of a light-colored material, but she could see little else of the structure. She lifted her gun arm, preparing for the worst. They crept forward side by side, placing each step with care as they approached the tree line.

Finding a good place to hide while observing their target, they stopped and squatted down. Before them, a large area cleared of vegetation surrounded the facility, the brown earth dried and cracked where it wasn't covered by crates or rovers closer to the building. It was a single structure, though she couldn't tell its shape from here. It had only one story and stretched off toward the trees in either direction, its smooth face interrupted only by windows and a single door. She accessed the Mission menu on her wrist comm and switched to a tech scan. On the HUD, a few security cameras were highlighted, as well as several automated turrets on the roof, but everything was offline.

Next, she switched to infrared, checking for signs of life. She pivoted her head back and forth, but the entire complex came up gray, with nothing lighting up whatsoever, not even a lowly piece of tech. No life forms. No power.

"What in the Nine Hells is going on here?"

Taln jerked her head to the side, shocked to hear Eirse's voice when they were supposed to be keeping a low profile.

"Eirse," she hissed under her breath.

"Relax. There's no one here. At least, there's no one I can detect with my sensors."

Taln sat down and leaned against a tree, the smooth bark pressing into her spine. "What scans did you run?"

"Tech scan and infrared." Eirse shrugged and sat down facing her, waving a hand toward the building. "There's tech there, but it's not under power, and I don't see any signs of life."

Taln looked over at the building, seeing it in a new light. It was the little details, really, that stood out to her now. The rover close to the building looked like it had been half packed before being abandoned, and one of the tires looked partially deflated. Far off to the right, a tree had fallen against the building, and it was currently being held in the air by a cable attached to an automated turret. There were crates waiting in the yard, as if a new shipment had arrived and they hadn't had time to deal with them yet. But when she zoomed in with her HUD, the wood appeared dark with rot close to the ground, and the metal brackets on the corners were rusted.

"It's abandoned," she said absently.

"That was my thoughts, as well. Waste of time."

Taln shook her head as she stood. "Not necessarily." She brushed dirt off her butt and holstered her weapon. "Just because it's abandoned doesn't mean it can't be useful to us. This was a black site, a facility so far off the beaten path nobody was expected to ever find it. They left things behind. If we're lucky, they left something useful."

"Should we head back? Gather more people?" Eirse asked, sounding like she didn't even want to suggest it.

Taln hid a smirk. "No, not yet. We still have horos before we're supposed to check in. Let's do a once over of the facility first. See what we're dealing with." She turned and looked back at Eirse, whose gaze shifted upward almost guiltily. "And keep your scanners on repeat. There's no telling what we're going to find in there, and just because we can't detect anything from out here doesn't mean there isn't something dangerous in there."

"Yes, ma'am."

They both reached for their wrist comms, and Taln selected "Repeat" from her scan options. That setting would loop through certain scans, only pausing when it detected something of significance, like an active security feed, body heat, or a live automated defense system.

In one smooth movement, Taln pulled her gun out and gave the command to advance with a hand gesture. Stepping out of the trees onto the hard, dry dirt, she moved swiftly toward the only visible entrance, Eirse on her heels. The door was made of a textured metal with a simple handle and an advanced security keypad to the right. She had the urge to curse when she spotted the keypad, but when she reached for the door, trying to decide how she would bypass the security, she found it ajar. She touched the edge with her fingertips, and was able to push it open with the barest of efforts, the hinges protesting audibly.

The interior of the building was dark, and she could only see to the first door down the corridor. She accessed her wrist comm and turned on the light feature. A beam of diffuse light flooded the hallway from her HUD, and a moment later, a second beam of light came from behind her. She stepped into the hallway, determined to show a calm demeanor in spite of the chills running down her back.

They moved through the facility, Taln remaining in the hallway while Eirse opened each door, clearing the building room by room. It took maybe an horo to clear the entire building, with only a single vault excluded from their search.

"We'll never get through that," Eirse said as they both stared at the large vault door at the center of the facility.

"Not in the..." Taln looked down at her comm. "...eleven horos we have until backup arrives." It would take an entire team of specialists the better part of an erno to even *try* to get inside that vault.

"Pity. I kinda wanna know what's in there."

"Well, you'll have to wait. We're not getting through that door today." She turned around, taking in the room, trying to decide its purpose. The building was laid out with housing and personnel support services on two wings and with work-spaces in this central hub. She wondered what they were working on. It was clear there were some biological components since some of the labs looked a bit like medical exam rooms. Eirse had also found syringes on her inspection of the rooms. This room, however, felt like the heart and brains of the facility, with workbenches dividing the center of the room, and computer banks lining the walls. So far, they'd found no paper files. "We need to get these computers up and running."

"You have a plan?"

"I don't know. At the moment, our best chance of figuring out what they were doing here is on those data banks."

"Okay. Why don't you look for a power generator, and I'll look for solar cells or fuel?"

Taln nodded. "Sounds good. I'm going to head back outside, check the cleared area for an outbuilding or something."

"I'm gonna check the roof for solar panels."

Taln nodded again, and they split up.

<hr>

As Eirse left the hub, she couldn't get over the feeling that she was being watched. She'd checked her scans again and again, and each time they said the same thing. Only she and Taln were in the building. And yet she couldn't shake the feeling like they weren't alone. It was starting to freak her out.

She was focused on reaching the roof access she'd spotted during their initial exploration of the building. Her hands never strayed far from her weapons, though, her steps rushed in her unease. She had an urge to keep a weapon in both hands at all times, but she resisted.

There is no threat.

No one's here.

But she didn't really believe that. She wasn't the superstitious sort, none of her people were, but they were also very practical. They *knew* the universe was bigger and more complex than anything they would ever experience personally. They *knew* they didn't know everything, and thus they didn't question when something seemingly impossible happened.

Like being watched when there were no live security feeds or signs of life.

Her hands gripped the cold metal rungs of the ladder bolted to the wall, and she quickly pulled herself up to the hatch in the ceiling, which required little more than a twist of her hand to unlock. She pushed, exposing the sky above. The hatch banged open, and she readjusted her grip, her fingers scraping against the coarse material of the roof. With a single pull, she lifted herself up, the material now irritating her feet instead.

Like many roofs all around the universe, this space was very utilitarian. The coarse material she'd felt when she'd pulled herself up was among the cheapest materials in the explored universe, but on a roof, no one cared. She slowly scanned around her, noting the various systems taking up space. Automated turrets, bundles of cables leading to security cameras and sensors, environmental control systems, a communications array, and off in the distance, solar panels.

Eirse crossed the roof quickly, wincing slightly at the rough material digging into her bare soles. She hated wearing shoes, finding them too restrictive, but in this instance, she almost wished she had them.

The solar panels covered the far wing of the building in rows. As she reached the great big black glassy slabs, she started checking for anything that might have caused them to stop working. Cables damaged or unplugged, damaged capacitors, surfaces shaded or marred by the elements. She walked through the rows, ducking down to check under each cell bank, checking its support struts and network of electronics before standing up again and checking the surface for damage. Each bank looked good, intact. Maybe a little dirty in places but unmarred. She didn't spot any indicators as to why there would be no power in the facility.

When she reached the last row, she turned around, taking in the long roof before her and the sun making its slow descent toward the horizon. The trees just barely reached above the lip of the roof, providing a clear view into the distance. There was something eerie about that vista, almost ominous.

Maybe it was the turrets quietly sitting sentinel in two parallel lines into the distance. She decided to tackle that next.

It wouldn't do, after all, to get power back online, then get taken out by the building's own security systems.

But before she could get started, she paused, looking around her as her instincts spoke up once more, demanding to be heard. What was it about this place that unnerved her so?

Maybe it was this sense of vast emptiness she couldn't quite shake. There was this feeling all of a sudden like almost nothing lived here, and in that moment, the world seemed disturbingly quiet. She couldn't hear a single creature, not even an insect. Just her own breathing and Taln moving around somewhere behind her. Even the trees themselves seemed to have held still, as if waiting for something to happen, something they were deathly afraid of.

And yet maybe it was the sunset itself. Symbolically, a sunset was an ending, though like with most endings, with the promise of a rebirth. And yet this sunset was different than most she'd experienced in her lifetime.

It was devoid of color.

Most sunsets included a variety of colors, ranging from the color of the relevant star to the natural color of the sky when the star was out of sight. At its most sedate, a sunset was usually a calming affair, a gentle visual transition from day to night. At its most vibrant, a sunset was a riot of colors splattered across the sky like an abstract painting. She'd never seen one like this before, though.

This sunset was strange, and for the first time, she realized several things. One: the star for this planet was a bright white, and she suspected it would be painful to look directly at in daylight. Two: the sky seemed to be a uniform gray, explaining the silvery surface to the water she'd seen earlier. And three: the moon was rising, just the barest swell above the treetops off to the left of the setting sun.

A chill ran down her spine again as she stared at that tiny glimpse of celestial rock. Some instinctual part of her feared its rising.

CHAPTER SIX

aln found the generator quickly enough, though she couldn't understand why it wasn't turned on. The day was drawing to a close as she moved about with intention, focusing on her mission. While they had plenty of horos until they needed to report in to the *Areon*, the setting star inspired a peculiar level of urgency in her.

In her investigation of the power situation, she'd already traced the lines leading out of the generator. Some lead to the roof, so Eirse was probably going to find solar panels up there. The rest just lead to the building, which made sense. What didn't make sense was that every line she checked looked intact. In fact, they were all high end power lines, designed to be used in the most brutal conditions. They couldn't be chewed or sawed through, and anything short of a detonation wasn't likely to do them any harm.

And yet, as she returned to the generator, it wasn't online. At first, she started looking for faults. Maybe a spark that had burned some sensitive electronics or a dent that might indicate some underlying damage. But it looked new. Dirty, but new. It had clearly been through a couple rainstorms, spatters of mud marring its surface, but it didn't have any of the obvious signs of wear and tear. No scratches from a tool slipping, no broken seals, no parts that looked older or newer than others. It was as if it had been installed direct from the manufacturer, then promptly abandoned.

After maybe half an horo of searching, she found nothing wrong with it. Looking for more information, she navigated to the Mission menu on her wrist comm, grateful Officer Sala had been thorough when she quickly pulled up specs and technical manuals on the generator before her. She scrolled to the troubleshooting section of the manual and found text that spelled out "Generator has shut off on its own."

The GenXT Rugged Power Station is designed to operate under all circumstances. To maximize performance and preserve the built-in capacitor and battery life, the power station will enter Low Power Mode when no power is drawn for greater than 3 ernos. During these Low Power Mode periods, the power station will power up again once battery charge drops below 50%. If no power is drawn from the power station for at least 6 morgos, it will enter Stasis Mode. See the Stasis Mode section of this Technical Manual for more details.

Taln quickly pulled up the relevant section.

5.1 Stasis Mode

Stasis Mode is intended to preserve the function of your new GenXT Rugged Power Station.

Running the station without drawing power for an extended period of time can cause damage to the unit's battery and capacitor. If you anticipate a prolonged period of disuse, you should activate the station's Stasis Mode to preserve function. You can access Stasis Mode by selecting the Stasis Mode icon from the GenXT app and following the prompts onscreen. Alternatively, the power station will enter Stasis Mode automatically when no power is drawn for 6 morgos.

The GenXT Rugged Power Station is also vulnerable to some classes of natural phenomenon, including lightning. When properly installed, the GenXT Sensor Array can accurately detect an imminent lightning strike in the area and trigger the activation of Stasis Mode to protect the unit.

Please consult your GenXT Sales Representative for guidance on how to protect your new GenXT Rugged Power Station from other natural phenomenon.

How to Exit Stasis Mode

You can exit Stasis Mode through the app by selecting the Stasis Mode icon or by selecting the red Stasis Mode button on the side of the station.

There was a diagram below. Taln followed it, finding a big, friendly red button on the side of the generator. Reaching out, she pressed it and the generator immediately kicked on with a gentle hum. She sat down on her butt, scratching her head in confusion.

What the hael happened here?

Eirse wandered back into the main hub feeling on edge. Everything was still offline. She even tried pressing a few power buttons, but nothing turned on. She glanced outside at the increasing darkness, the trees little more than shadows at this point. Taln still hadn't returned, and her stomach was starting to twist with anxiety.

Was something wrong?

Should she go out there after her? Back her up?

Deep down, some instinctual part of her *knew* there was something very wrong with this place, but she honestly couldn't put her finger on it. She started to suspect spending so much time in space had done her no favors, like maybe some sense she should be listening to had withered with disuse, leaving her with only the nagging impression of danger, too vague and undirected to provide any benefit.

Eirse growled in frustration, turning away from the vista beyond the windows. She started pacing back and forth across the room. When Taln finally walked through the far doorway, she stopped and changed directions. "About time," she said.

"Power should be up now. Let's see what they're hiding."

Eirse watched as Taln approached the bank of computers on the far wall. "What do you think we'll find?" she asked, pausing behind her to appreciate the view.

Nine Depths, that's a fine ass.

"No idea. They were clearly experimenting on people, though."

"And they didn't use their shuttle to leave. They just abandoned it there."

Taln turned around, her hands hovering over an input device. "Maybe it got damaged, and they needed to call headquarters to come get them?"

"Maybe." But Eirse didn't quite buy that. There was just something so ominous about their circumstances, something that whispered to her that nothing here was what it seemed.

"Start booting the computers up."

"Yes, Captain," Eirse said, reluctantly leaving Taln's side to boot each computer one by one, her mind elsewhere.

She actually hated that her mind was split between worrying about their situation and worrying about her chances with her captain. On the one hand, she needed to be on top of her game. She had the nagging feeling that the eerily quiet facade of this place would soon be ripped away to reveal its dark underbelly.

On the other, though, her logical mind told her to just trust what she could see and hear. Everything was quiet. She had no reason to think this facility was anything but abandoned.

And yet, with those two sides warring against each other and taking up so much of her focus, how could she possibly find the time to seduce Taln? It just seemed impossible. They had so little time here until they had to head back. With how she'd thrown herself at Taln in the past without the other woman being the wiser, she was almost hesitant to approach her. What in the Nine Depths was it going to take to get it to click in Taln's head that Eirse wanted more?

Should she just say it?

Taln, I want to be your girlfriend.

Taln, I like you.

Taln, I want to drag you to bed and not come up for air for ernos.

They all sounded good… and equally difficult to actually say. It was easy enough in her head. Thoughts tended to flow as easily as water, but words? Real spoken words? They tended to get tangled on your tongue or stuck in your throat. Sometimes, you meant one thing and said something entirely different. Other times, you said exactly what you meant, but the other person heard something entirely different.

Maybe I should just kiss her or something.

That could work. No questioning what *that* meant. And it might be easier than speaking her mind. Just get up a little courage, walk up to her, and kiss her. No words. No second guessing herself. Just do it.

She looked over at Taln. Taln just stood there, leaning over the desk and staring at the screen. Her back was straight, her ass outlined perfectly in those pants. Even the camo couldn't hide their perfect shape, or the way the backs of her legs pressed against the material. She also had this intense look on her face that made her look all serious and adorable. Eirse wanted nothing more than to walk up behind her and wrap her arms around her, resting her chin on her shoulder like a couple who'd been together for alos.

She resisted the urge to sigh.

Focus, stupid. You have work to do.

Eirse returned her gaze to the computer she was sitting at, her elbow on the desk, cheek propped on her fist. It had finished booting, showing a log in screen. This was the moment of truth, she supposed. The Diehli were pretty big in the security business. She couldn't imagine them being vulnerable to most forms of intrusion. She could… see if the software on her wrist comm could bypass the log in screen—she gave that a 50-50 chance at best—or see if her old credentials still worked.

Eirse doubted they would be stupid enough to leave her credentials active after she'd defected to Inia, but you never knew. Things could slip through the cracks sometimes. She entered her information and waited.

A moment later, the display changed to the operating system's desktop, a generic screen with a few icons and menu options. She smirked, allowing herself a little happy dance in her seat, then started exploring the computer.

The first thing she noticed was that it was currently offline, an icon on the bottom right corner cycling as it tried again and again to make a connection. She clicked it and set it to Offline Mode, then checked the log to see when it had last connected to the network.

Her jaw dropped slightly when she saw the date. It was from before she'd left Diehli. "Um, Taln, when was that equipment ordered and delivered here?"

"I don't remember. Let me check."

Eirse waited as Taln accessed her wrist comm. "Roughly three alos ago."

"So maybe before I left."

Taln looked over at her. "Yes, it would have been delivered a couple morgos before you joined Inia. Why?

"My credentials still work. This computer hasn't connected to the network since before I left Diehli."

Taln crossed her arms. "Hm. I don't know if that's a boon or not. If that's when this place was abandoned, then they couldn't have accomplished much, making this mission a bust. Just an old facility left fallow."

Eirse leaned forward. "Maybe not. I mean why did they abandon it after only a few morgos? And why did they set it up all the way out here? There's a secret here. It may be nothing or it may be huge, but it was certainly important to them. They put a lot of money into building this facility out here, and you don't do that for nothing."

"Yeah, that was my thoughts as well when Sala first gave me this intel." She walked over to Eirse, hovering over her shoulder. "Since you're already logged in, what else have you got?"

Eirse paused for a moment, her eyes closed as she savored their proximity. She could almost *feel* Taln's body heat. "Nothing yet," she said on an out-breath, trying to refocus on the computer before her.

She pulled up the file directory, searching for clues. The organization of the drive felt fairly familiar, a lot like what she'd seen back at Diehli headquarters. But this was a research facility, so there was also a lot she didn't recognize. She started idly clicking.

Users

Security

Projects

The projects folder seemed the most promising, but it also made her feel the most out of her depths. There was only one folder under projects. *89058 Shadow.*

Nine Hells. Even the folders are ominous here.

She clicked it. A list of names. Were they subjects? Scientists? She clicked one. Scientists, she decided. A folder titled "Subjects" was below this folder, and she clicked it. Each subject was assigned a numbered folder. She clicked the first one. It contained only a series of date-stamped files of various types.

Most were text files, but others were video or audio. She suspected the rest were exports from scientific equipment. She clicked the first text file.

Subject 89058-001 arrived today via shuttle. Consent forms read and signed. First dose of AS058 administered at 08:47.

She closed out the file and opened one much farther down.

Physical exam completed of subject 89058-001. Results are not ideal. Suspect a new variant will need to be created for future subjects.

Eirse backed out of that folder and proceeded to another folder, clicking the first text file. She noted that the first entry was half a morgo later.

Subject 89058-037 arrived yesterday. Consent forms read and signed. First dose of KS058 administered at 06:28. May need to adjust subject housing. This one seems hostile.

She scrolled down, picking something farther down again.

Fifth dose of KS058 administered at 14:49. Testing has confirmed subject 89058-037 has no control, like previous subjects. Archiving variant KS058.

Eirse flipped through folder after folder, file after file. They were all the same. Different, but the same. "They're testing some sort of serum on people. And it wasn't getting the results they wanted. And from the looks of it, it *wasn't* working *really* fast. The date range of all these subject files only spans maybe a morgo or two." She turned around to Taln. "If I'm reading this right, they had dozens of subjects, probably filling this entire facility. And by my guess, they went through a lot of iterations of this serum. I counted at least five, but based on the naming structure, I'd say there were nearly a dozen."

Taln frowned.

"And there was something about phasing. I kept reading that, but I'm not sure what it means. A lot of the files mentioned a lack of control, too."

"Keep on it."

She nodded. "Yes, ma'am."

CHAPTER SEVEN

"Keep on it," Taln said as she straightened.

Eirse nodded. "Yes, ma'am."

"I'm going to do a deeper dive of the facility. See if I can find anything that will give us a hint as to what they were trying to do here."

"I don't think that's a good idea." There was a look of alarm in her eyes, one she'd never seen in the other woman before.

"There's no one here. It'll be fine."

"That's not what I meant," Eirse said, leaning farther forward.

"And what did you mean?"

"Can't you feel it? There's something wrong with this place."

"Like what?"

"Well, there's this mystery, first off. Why did they leave? What were they doing? Why does it feel like they just disappeared?"

"There's no reason to believe they 'just disappeared.' Like I said before, they probably just called for a ride back to headquarters after the shuttle was destroyed."

"Then why didn't they take anything with them? There's a lot of expensive equipment here, and it was all left to rot. Those automated turrets *alone* would be worth a small fortune on the black market. There's got to be at least a dozen of them up there, but the *Diehli* never came back to claim them." Eirse stared Taln down, her next words feeling like a personal attack. "How long has this facility been abandoned?"

Taln felt uncomfortable with the question. Eirse's tone said it all. That sexy, confident air that Taln loved so much now felt like a bad thing. It left her in an awkward position, wedged between Eirse's knowing gaze and her own unwillingness to acknowledge the nagging suspicion at the back of her mind. "At least six morgos, maybe a few alos," she said, feeling like a child admitting to a wrongdoing.

Eirse scoffed. "More than enough time to come back and salvage things. And what about the damage to that shuttle? What did that? It wasn't a person.

"And why is it that when night started to settle and the moon started to rise, suddenly all the animals got quiet?"

"It was most likely a local predator. And if we went outside right now, the animals would probably be making noise again. There's nothing to worry about. All the doors are closed, power is back online. No animals are getting in here."

Eirse looked at her like she'd just insisted that 2+2=5.

"It'll be fine. And we have our wrist comms." She lifted her wrist and reactivated wireless transmissions. "If I need help, I can ask for it, and you're only a few rooms away."

Then she had a thought, and she looked up from her comm, pointing at the monitor next to Eirse. "Check and see if the computer has a comms log. Maybe we can find out what happened based on their communications off-planet."

Eirse nodded, but didn't look happy about it.

Taln walked away, determined to prove there was nothing to be afraid of. As she stepped into the first of the exam rooms, it struck her as so strange that Eirse would fear anything at all. She was normally either eager or practical in dangerous situations, but something about this mission was throwing her off her game. As her superior, Taln wanted to reassure her, to pump her up and give her the confidence to get the job done, but she also just wanted to hug her and tell her everything would be okay, which was totally inappropriate.

The room was similar to any basic medical suite. Cabinets and tools on the walls, a sink, receptacles for waste, and a bed in the center of the room. She started going through the cupboards, looking for clues. Mostly, the contents were pretty standard. Gauze, syringes, a vital stats cuff.

The only surprise in the entire search was discovering that one of the cupboards was actually a refrigerator. It contained bottles of liquid labeled only with LS058, a manufacture date, and an expiration date, as well as what seemed to be some sedatives, though the name on the label was some long-assed string of letters she was fairly positive wasn't a real word.

There was almost nothing else, and she still had no idea what they'd been doing in this room.

She found little of interest as she moved through exam room after exam room, a few labs (with more of the aforementioned little bottles of mystery liquid), and some office space. There weren't any papers lying around or any obvious hints as to what the cryptically titled LS058 truly was.

Even back on the *Areon* when she'd gone over all the shipping manifests, she'd found nothing other than an overall trend of medical-related equipment. Nothing gave away their true purpose here. It was starting to get frustrating.

Honestly, the only thing noteworthy about the entire search was the number of times she'd thought she'd caught movement out of the corner of her eye, only for there to be nothing there.

And she attributed *those* paranoid figments of her imagination to Eirse's minor freak out right before they'd parted.

Done with the main hub, Taln stepped into the hallway leading toward one of the residential wings. With nothing to distract her, the unnatural silence of the place started to get to her. It was so quiet, she would have thought she'd lost her sense of hearing if not for her soft breaths every few moments or the constant tapping of her boots against the floor.

Tink.

She spun around, certain she'd heard something behind her, a sharp tap, clear as day.

There was nothing there.

"Eirse?" she asked, not expecting an answer. The hall was just as empty and quiet as before.

She turned around slowly, hesitant to turn her back on what was probably just her mind playing tricks on her. She'd been in enough dangerous situations, though, to never take that for granted.

Taln stepped quieter after that, but only heard her own movements through the space. The hall transitioned to the residential wing, and it was like night and day… literally. The main hub had open doors and late evening rays coming through a plethora of windows, but here? Nothing. She reached forward, fortunately just barely able to see an illumination panel on the wall to her right. With a single tap, the bulbs flickered, then came on, giving off just enough light to see the numbers assigned to each room. Each door was closed.

As she continued down the hall, she checked each room. Most were locked tight. She had to try four doors before the fifth opened, exposing a living quarters that didn't look quite right. There was a single window on the opposite wall letting in weak light from the setting sun, giving a sinister quality to the space, but that wasn't what unnerved her so. No, it was the way it seemed like the owner of this room might return at any moment.

The bed was made, but rumpled, like they'd sat on it after making it up. There were clean clothes in a hamper waiting to be put away. On a table in the corner, there was a bowl and utensil waiting next to a box of breakfast food, like the resident had intended it for their next meal. A thick layer of dust covered the bowl.

On the table next to the bed, a tablet had been placed there, like they'd set it to charge before bed. She tried to power it up, but the battery was dead.

Something moved in her peripheral vision again, and she jerked to her side, stumbling and falling against the bed as she pulled her gun out of reflex. Her hand shook as she scanned the room once more, but it was empty.

"You're being ridiculous," she scolded herself. "There's nothing here."

And yet she couldn't quite convince herself of that, her mind straying once more to her conversation with Eirse.

"Can't you feel it? There's something wrong with this place," Eirse had said. She didn't want to admit it, but she was starting to agree.

Eirse was simultaneously worried and annoyed as she watched Taln walk away. The more time passed, the more she was certain something terrible had happened here, and that the threat might still be present.

The distance and the unknown frayed at her nerves. At least with Taln in sight, they could tackle the danger together, like they had on Wesa.

She smiled. It was still fresh in her mind how perfectly they'd fought in sync. It had been beautiful, like something out of a movie.

Which brought her to the reason she was also *annoyed*. Here she'd hoped to use this mission as an opportunity to show Taln once and for all how she felt, maybe even seduce her, and they weren't even in the same room. True, this wasn't the first time they'd separated since the mission started, but she was starting to feel the passage of time. The horos were slipping away, and soon enough, they would be back on the *Areon*, and she would be right back where she started, helplessly pining over the woman.

She needed to act, and she needed to do it soon.

Eirse frowned and turned back to her computer screen. "Comms log… right." She returned to the main screen, searching for some communications software. In the lower right corner, she spotted the stylized bird icon for Falcom Technologies and clicked it. It was the same software they'd used back at headquarters, so finding the comms log was a breeze.

She had to change some settings, but soon she had a log of all the communications in and out of this facility from the moment the software was installed. Time- and date-stamps lined a column on the left, followed by ID numbers for each sender or receiver. Some of them were encrypted, with one or both IDs scrambled. It listed durations of calls, the station that sent or received it, and an icon for accessing recordings of all non-encrypted calls and messages, which required a password.

The last entry was only a few morgos after the first, confirming what she'd already suspected. This facility had barely been up and running before something shut it down for good.

Eirse leaned back in her chair, rubbing her scars as she tried to think of what to investigate next. She was *sure* the facility was never evacuated, but how could she prove it?

She closed the Falcom software and searched for the security suite she'd used back at headquarters. Unlike Falcom, it was in-house, with just an image of a lock as the icon and the word "Security" underneath it. She clicked it. The familiar welcome screen came up, with a column of bright red warnings running down the right side of the screen, flashing annoyingly as they complained that the turrets were offline. She silenced them, and they settled, instead just showing red boxes with "Turret Offline" inside each one.

Eirse was surprised by the quantity of security here. For a place like this, she'd expected a few cameras, maybe just enough to monitor the entrances and the central hub. When she pulled up the Feed screen, however, she found that there wasn't a single place within the tree line that wasn't under some sort of surveillance.

Not interested in the active feeds, she clicked Archive at the bottom of the screen, and it brought up a calendar. Each erno that contained data would be shaded in. The entire screen showed morgos of dates that had no surveillance data, all except today. She moved further back, looking for the last date with data. Each screen showed only about four morgos, so she had to scroll back several times before she found more shaded dates.

When she found one, she clicked the most recent, but she didn't need to check it very thoroughly to know there was nothing to see. Not a single motion detector in the entire facility registered movement. All the auditory monitors showed no spikes in volume. The facility was abandoned. It was probably right before the generator powered down for good.

She didn't know how long the generator had sat idle before shutting down, so she quickly ran through the next few ernos of data. Two more ernos were completely empty. No motion. No audio.

Then she found something. The fourth erno back had motion and an increase in volume. As she suspected, when she hit play on the audio, choosing an especially high peak on the graph, she didn't hear the sounds of people evacuating or shutting down a defunct facility. Even so, she still wasn't prepared for what she did hear.

Screams.

People were screaming…

Once she'd finished with the one residential wing, Taln crossed to the other side of the facility to check out the other one. She immediately discovered a difference. This side of the facility was much nicer. Lights turned on automatically. There were windows in the hallway, and when she managed to open a door, the quarters were several-fold larger and far better equipped.

"This must be staff quarters," she muttered under her breath as she entered the first room. This room had a larger bed and a nice office area off to the left. Taln walked over to the desk, smiling when she finally discovered some documentation. Every other place she'd looked had given nothing away, but this looked like it might be the start of some answers.

The desk was messy, like the owner had been in a rush, or maybe this was their natural state, ordered chaos. There was a tablet on the edge of the surface, a computer monitor at the back, writing instruments strewn about carelessly across the surface, a pair of reading glasses sitting on their lenses, and the corners of several pieces of paper peeking out of a drawer. It would have been easy to miss in their initial check of the facility.

When she pulled it open, the drawer was filled with papers. Some were in notebooks, but much of it was loose. She pulled them all out and spread them across the desktop before scanning through the pile, pushing pieces aside with her fingertips. It didn't immediately make a cohesive picture of what they were working on.

Moving on from the loose sheets of paper, she started picking up the notebooks. They were all similar. Hard navy blue backing with lined pages inside and about two hand-spans tall. She flipped through the first few, but only found chemical formulas and scientific jargon she couldn't possibly decipher.

Should have brought a scientist on this mission.

Except she hadn't expected to get this far. She'd figured they would touch down, approach the facility, get a feel for their security, then regroup. She hadn't expected it to be abandoned, and that meant neither of them was really the best person for the job. Eirse was a great person to have at your back in a conflict, but she wasn't much of an investigator, at least not on this level. She knew security, fighting, and people.

She knew how people thought and what they might do when stressed. In that way, she could be a fantastic investigator, but this was all going through documents and searching for clues, not searching for people.

They were both out of their depths.

But then she opened a book that was different. It seemed to be a journal, though it looked the same on the outside. As she started to read, it contained a mix of personal and professional observations, and she sat down at the desk to skim through it.

She flipped through the section where the person detailed the founding of the facility, setting everything up and such. After that, there were passages talking about the experiments, the constant failures.

I'm dismayed by our lack of progress. We are now on the fifth variant of recombinant DNA therapy and yet still no success. The subjects show no more sign of being able to control the phasing than during the first trials. What are we doing wrong?

Taln paused after reading that. DNA? She looked away from the book, taking in her surroundings once more, seeing it in a new light. "This isn't some serum. They were changing people." The journal in her hands suddenly felt weighty, like it was a dark confession of many sins. Most planets banned that type of technology for anything but treating genetic diseases.

She shook her head. "Why am I surprised?" The Diehli had built their entire empire outside of any government's territory for the very purpose of ensuring they could do whatever they wanted. Of course, they were going to do things most governments found reprehensible.

And yet, it still disturbed her.

Her mind shying away from the potential horrors of this place, she flipped forward again, ignoring the information about experiments, instead focusing on figuring out why they'd left. She found the last entry somewhere around halfway through the pages. It stopped mid-sentence, the handwriting getting a little erratic near the end.

I shouldn't even be writing this, but I need to think and journaling clears my mind.

It's not safe here anymore, not since the moon started to rise again. We figured it out too late. They've become too aggressive, their numbers too great. We shouldn't have ignored the warning signs. We shouldn't have assumed we were safe.

The screaming calls from outside have grown so loud now. It sends chills down my spine. Oh, how I miss my former ignorance. I know what those screams mean now. Just yesterday, it meant the destruction of our shuttle.

We can't escape. I know that now. We would be long dead before help arrived, and even the far nearer salvation of dawn seems completely out of reach.

Gods, they are so aggressive now. They will not stop until they get to us. We have only one chance of survival, but it is our own downfall as much as a salvation. Gods help

---

Taln leaned back in her seat, the journal dropping to her lap. They never left.

She shook her head. "But then, where are they?"

Eirse felt almost sick to her stomach with nerves after hearing those screams on the audio. She'd half wanted to either rush out of the hub searching for Taln or call her on her comm, but she resisted both urges.

The room seemed to close in around her the longer she was alone, and the feeling of being watched intensified. She started seeing things out of the corner of her eyes, but when she turned, there was never anything there. At one point, she could have sworn something on one of the countertops had moved, but was her mind playing tricks on her?

Maybe Taln was right. Maybe she was overreacting. Maybe she needed to spend more time planetside. It *had* been a long time since she'd last had some true-gravity time. She spent so much time on ships and space stations nowadays that she supposed it was possible her senses were just overreacting to the normal stimuli that existed in an uncontrolled environment.

The native wildlife *could* have reacted to a predator by quieting, and she *could* have imagined that movement she thought she'd seen, and she *could* have been mistaken when she thought something had moved on that workstation.

"Everything's fine." She shrugged. "And even if it isn't, you can handle it."

Relaxing a little, she returned her gaze to the computer screen, but she didn't have it in her to go deeper into the surveillance at the moment. Her nerves were a bit too frayed, and the sound of those screams was still ringing through her psyche.

So instead, she leaned back, staring at the plain white ceiling. "Maybe instead of freaking out over nothing, I should be focusing on deciding how to approach Taln."

But it seemed impossible. What-ifs kept teasing the edges of her mind, tormenting her with possible scenarios that would make life on the *Areon* impossibly awkward afterwards. All her team was rooting for her to win Taln over, but what if they were wrong? What if this all went horribly awry? What if she put herself out there and Taln coldly told her no?

"No, you're not going down this route," she said, shaking herself, then standing to pace the room between the rows of workstations. "That type of thinking does not solve anything. Instead, you need to just not think about it. No practiced words, no speeches, just do it."

She was psyching herself up, forcing all possible negative repercussions from her mind, her movements becoming faster, almost frantic as she paced.

When footsteps sounded from down the hall, she jumped, jerking her head up in surprise. Her mouth hung open as she waited, unable to move. There were several long moments of anticipation and fear, where she didn't know if it was her captain or something more sinister striding down the hallway.

But when Taln's familiar form slipped into view, she suddenly fell into action. She no longer felt in control of her own body as she crossed the space. Taln wasn't paying attention, her gaze at first going to the computer console where she expected Eirse to be. Her crush was just starting to turn her head when Eirse arrived, thrust her hands forward like snakes striking, and pulled her close, the silky texture of her buzz cut tickling her fingers. She leaned in, her mouth touching paradise, and sighed, feeling as if she'd arrived home after being lost for far too long. Without conscious thought, she melted into the kiss.

Her entire body was heating up, leaving her breathless and half insensate. She had no sense of time as the kiss went on. And she didn't care.

Until their lips started moving in concert. *That* brought her back to herself. It surprised her at first, and she gasped, but then she renewed the kiss, pressing deeper.

Finally, she thought as she smiled against Taln's lips, taking the mutual kiss as the answer she craved.

CHAPTER EIGHT

"*E*irse, what the hael?" Taln said as she pulled back in surprise. She stumbled, bumping into the doorframe.

And yet, even with that distance, she could still feel the ghost of Eirse's lips pressed against her own. The girl in her wanted to touch her lips in wonder, but the captain in her couldn't believe what had just transpired.

This can't happen.

She stood there, breathing heavily as she tried to wrangle her chaotic thoughts.

That was unprofessional, she told herself. *She's a subordinate. I shouldn't have done that. I should have pulled back immediately.*

And yet she hadn't, and for several long moments, that's all she could think of. Long moments with their lips moving together. Long moments where Eirse's leaner swimmer's build leaned up against her own. If she hadn't been so surprised, she might have actually reached out and held her, pulled her close.

But this is wrong.

She took in and released a deep, steadying breath, then smoothed a hand over her hair and adjusted her camo shirt, which unfortunately didn't have the same effect as straightening her shipboard uniform. She cleared her throat and finally returned her focus to Eirse.

Eirse looked gutted, spinning around and muttering some excuse to escape as she rushed out of the room, slamming the door behind her.

"Well, I could have handled that better."

<hr>

"Fuck, fuck, fuck," Eirse said, using a human term she'd learned from Cass. It just rolled off her tongue, perfectly expressing her feelings of the moment. "Oh, fuck."

For several diceros, she had no idea where she was going. She wasn't seeing the hallway. She was only running. Running away from her mistake. Running away from Taln and her inevitable judgment.

By the time she stopped panicking and looked up to see where she was going, she was already in one of the residential wings. She stopped in front of a big floor-to-ceiling window at the end of a hall and stared out at the world beyond. The sun was still making its slow descent, making her realize just how little time had truly passed since they'd arrived. She wasn't sure how long the ernos were here or how long twilight lasted, but there was still light in the sky, too much light to be just reflected sunlight against the moon.

Feeling defeated, she slumped against the wall and slid to the floor. "Oh," she said, holding her face in her hands, "that went about as badly as possible." The way Taln had just yanked away from her kept replaying in her mind, taunting her with a visceral feeling of rejection.

She lifted her head and laughed. Which was weird because the urge to cry was almost overwhelming. "This is just what I deserve, isn't it? All that time working for Diehli?" She shook her head and sniffed, tears welling in her eyes. "All the things I did," she whispered. Even alone, even without giving any details, she still couldn't say it any louder. It almost broke her soul now to think about it. How could she have let herself fall so far? "I made my bed and now I'm, apparently, stuck in it." She sniffed again, and a single tear rolled down her cheek.

Suddenly, homesickness swept over her like mad, and more tears poured from her eyes. Crying was different back home in the sea. You didn't feel it, not like this. You could feel the emotion, feel your face heating as blood rushed to your skin, but when the tears finally came, they were washed away, allowing you a modicum of dignity.

"Oh, I miss it so much," she said, her voice thick with everything she was feeling. She took in a shaky breath and let it out. "Why did it have to happen? Why was that predator there? Why couldn't I save them?" The questions kept coming, bombarding her with what-ifs and guilt. Eirse blamed herself for throwing that spear, blamed herself for not telling her partner to flee or hide. *She'd* snared the predator. *She'd* put her partner in danger.

And they'd both paid the price.

She shook her head. "Nothing's been right since." First, dealing with the aftermath. The injury, recovery, judgment, facing her hunting partner's family, trying to find normalcy again, failing, trying to start over somewhere new, and failing at that, too.

Then, there was the Diehli. She'd left her homeworld because she couldn't take it anymore. People had looked at her with pity, and she couldn't blame them. She'd been a drain on society. She'd wanted to help, but she could barely swim. After the "accident," she'd needed to feel useful, but what use was a Tursiops who couldn't swim properly?

That and the guilt had driven her off-world.

But the guilt and self-loathing hadn't eased just because she'd left her home behind. She'd felt useless, with no valuable skills to speak of, and as such, she'd felt unworthy of the opportunities she came across. She'd started out with a few low-end jobs, things that needed no skill sets or had no prerequisites. They'd been fine, but she'd felt out of place, disconnected from her coworkers. She didn't feel like she belonged, so she always ended up leaving in search of something else.

Eventually, she found Diehli. She hadn't, at first, known of the Diehli's reputation. She'd just taken yet another entry-level job. The difference, though, was apparent almost immediately. With the other jobs, she'd felt like an outsider. She'd been able to *feel* how the other workers seemed to bond while she stood on the outside looking in. But at Diehli? The entire atmosphere was different. There was no camaraderie. People didn't invite coworkers for luncheons or parties. The business didn't hold social events and get-togethers. At Diehli, it was everyone for themselves. Connections were made for common advantage and nothing more. Backstabbing was pretty much expected, both literally and figuratively.

Diehli was simultaneously alarming and refreshing. It wasn't home, it certainly wasn't comforting, but at least there were no pretenses. Everyone knew you could trust no one, so you didn't bother. You didn't make friends. You looked out for number one. It felt like the best she could hope for after everything that had happened. At least there, she'd had *something* in common with the people around her. Being disconnected had felt normal, not belonging had felt normal. She could embrace that solitary nature and prove herself in maybe the only way left to her, which had the added benefit of protecting herself in the process.

But in truth, if she was being honest with herself, she'd stayed at Diehli because she couldn't imagine someplace better. She'd let herself do things, unspeakable things, because she'd convinced herself she was a terrible person. She'd believed she belonged there. Maybe she'd seen it as some sort of penance, but looking back, there was no way to know for sure. All she knew was she'd never given herself a chance to imagine something better. Every doubt had been wiped away with some new excuse, some new imagined flaw, until even the worst sins seemed normal.

And now I have to live with that.

She banged the back of her head against the wall in defeat. "I don't deserve Taln. No wonder she rejected me."

As she stared out the window, feeling like the world was ending, she realized the sun had officially set.

It felt like an ending, and the urge to cry intensified.

Taln spent several long diceros staring at that door after Eirse left the room, wishing she could have handled that better. "I could have been gentler. I could have tried to explain." She crossed the room and stared out at the approaching night. "I could have told her why. It wouldn't have even been that hard.

"You're my subordinate. It wouldn't be appropriate." And yet, for the first time, that excuse didn't seem good enough. It *felt* wrong, wanting Eirse, craving her, but technically, it was allowed. Inia Intergalactic didn't have any rules against fraternization. Hael, there were even rules about how to handle it professionally.

So why was she so stuck on the idea that being with Eirse would be wrong? Why was she so stuck on the idea that she needed to be this perfect, professional employee at all times?

Taln supposed part of it came down to her past. She'd grown up an alien orphan, coming of age and joining the workforce on a planet that gave priority to natives. So, even though she'd lived there almost her entire life, she'd been an outsider in the eyes of employers, and she'd had to watch as opportunity after opportunity passed her by. Eventually, Attrition Services, the program that weaned people off government assistance, started threatening to cut her off. Taln received notices that her eligibility would expire on her next birthday, a date rapidly approaching. She was frustrated and overwhelmed, feeling like she'd never had a chance. That stupid deadline was designed with natives in mind, and because of that, she was about to age out of the program. And if she didn't find a job soon, she would be out on the streets.

Looking back, her life before starting with Inia had been fraught with uncertainty. She'd constantly survived at the mercy of others, and that was why she'd appreciated Inia so much. It was her first shot, the first time she'd been allowed to *earn* her place rather than being a burden nobody wanted.

And she had. Taln had worked hard, earning everything she'd received. She'd quickly worked her way up to captain, and knew both the owner, Inia Surg, and his brother and current company president, Varn, personally. She'd received instructions directly from them in the past, including her current assignment to help take down the Diehli. And she supposed she attributed at least some of that success to her calm demeanor and staunch professionalism.

And yet, she realized as the sun's light faded away into darkness, she had nothing outside of her job. It was her life. It was what gave her meaning and purpose. She didn't know what she was outside of it, and she supposed she'd never even tried to figure it out. The job… she could control. The job… she could rely on. Everything else was uncertain and just the tiniest bit terrifying.

Taln turned away from the window, no longer wanting to dwell on these darker thoughts. She didn't need to. There were more important things to focus on, like what they would do next.

She pulled the journal out of her back pocket and sat at one of the consoles. Staring at the notebook for several diceros, she tried to reorganize her thoughts. What happened after the events of the journal? They were afraid and convinced they wouldn't survive the night.

But they'd also had a solution. She checked the date on the last entry, then faced the computer where Eirse was still logged in. She was even logged into the surveillance software. Taln smiled wryly. "We do think alike, now don't we?"

On the screen, she selected the date from the entry, which brought up all the surveillance data for that erno. Audio, video, motion sensors, turret statuses, and alarms on doors and windows. She checked the motion sensors first, looking for the last readings. It would give her somewhere to start.

From there, she moved to video, choosing a point half an horo before the last motion. She selected videos for the hub, residential hallways, and set the labs and medical suites to rotate through.

What she found was chaos.

People were running around in a panic. She could tell they were yelling even though the audio was not on by default. Several individuals seemed calmer, directing traffic, coordinating efforts. Someone left the hub and rushed into one of the medical suites, grabbing things from the cabinets there, then returned. They addressed the crowd, holding up something too small to see on the screen she was using. Slowly, the items were distributed and the once hectic crowd settled down, looking resigned and defeated.

They lifted their sleeves, and soon she realized what was going on. They were injecting themselves with the experimental formula, the one every source they'd found so far indicated was flawed.

Then something startled the crowd, and they all jumped. Panic ensued once more, with leaders trying to get everyone to calm down again, but it was no use. The threat had arrived, and everyone knew it. Whatever hope they'd received from the formula vanished and then something changed. The frenzy increased. People tried to flee. They were running away, but from what?

Blood splattered the room on screen, and she jumped. "What?" What was that? She paused the video, backed it up, and played it again. She saw more this time and even slowed the playback speed down so she could really catch every detail. Anticipation and a little bit of dread filled her as she watched, knowing what was about to happen. And even though she was prepared, she still jumped when the injuries formed a moment before blood sprayed the room.

"That's impossible," she whispered under her breath.

Were her eyes playing tricks on her?

Was it some special effects or an elaborate illusion?

She wanted to say yes, but the footage had come directly from the security system. How could it have been altered?

And yet she couldn't deny what she'd seen. It was plain as day right there in front of her. There'd been no attacker, just a shadow with no source, there and then gone. Like a horror from a nightmare, the shadow had come, left a bloody path of destruction, then disappeared.

Her heart pounded in her chest as the video continued to play out. Her breathing was just the slightest bit erratic, and she couldn't really see what happened after that. It was too much. It was impossible. Any yet, she couldn't deny it was very much real.

Eirse had been right. There *was* something wrong with this place, and she'd just seen it with her own two eyes.

CHAPTER NINE

When Eirse walked back through the door, Taln noticed an odd tinge to her cheeks, her entire face looking just a little different than normal. She couldn't place it, just knew it was different.

"Eirse?"

She looked up, seeming a bit alarmed. Taln gave her a moment to compose herself, knowing the importance of appearances.

When Eirse looked back at her again, she *should* have told her what she'd seen on the video. She *should* have started a discussion on the tactics and strategies involved in handling murderous shadows, but those things had completely slipped her mind. In fact, what *did* come out seemed to spring from her head fully formed, with no forethought whatsoever. "How could you?"

The words surprised her almost from the moment they slipped from her mouth, yet she couldn't take them back, and she realized she didn't want to. She realized for the first time since that kiss that she felt betrayed by Eirse's actions. At first, she'd just felt shock. She hadn't expected it and had pulled away, not knowing how to deal with it.

But now she was coming to know there was more to it than that. She'd held out *hope* toward Eirse even while she'd ignored her own desires. Eirse was raw and real, shaped by her past as much as Taln was, but she seemed to have weathered it beautifully. She was confident, and that had bled into their interactions together. She constantly bucked authority, but that also meant she didn't kowtow to it either. If she deigned to be around you, it was because she wanted to be. And frankly, she was more likely to sneer at Taln's perfectionist issues than applaud them. She never failed to say when she was displeased, and while Taln still didn't know how to deal with that, at least there was no uncertainty there.

"What?" Eirse said, her eyes narrowed in confusion. Her voice was thick and the words, "How could you?" continued to linger between them, a problem neither of them knew how to address.

Unable to take the words back, Taln decided to run with it. She didn't know what she was doing. This was an unprecedented situation, something she'd tried to avoid her entire life, but for once, her first instinct wasn't to bury it all deep inside and pretend it didn't exist. Instead, she let it all out, giving voice to the deluge of feelings waiting to boil out of her. "The kiss, Eirse." She shook her head. "How could you? It was selfish. You… you… you didn't even give me a choice. You clearly weren't thinking about *me* and what *I* wanted, just your own wants and needs."

"I…"

Taln pointed at her. "No, let me finish. You didn't ask. You didn't ask how I felt. You didn't ask what I wanted. You just took. You didn't think for a *moment* whether I wanted that kiss, and you gave me no chance to react. Just *bam*, kiss, and then

I'm expected to know what to do with that. How did you expect me to react?"

"I'm sorry. I shouldn't have done that."

"You're right. You shouldn't have. You should have asked." *I might have said yes.*

Taln looked away, realizing in her irritation she wasn't being fair to Eirse. No, she probably *wouldn't* have said yes, if she was being honest with herself. She probably would have cited professionalism and propriety as an excuse not to get her heart involved.

And was that it? Was she just scared to get her heart involved, to try for something that didn't have clear rules and expectations? Relationships were messy, nebulous, and the path to success was often hard to see. And though, in theory, there should be more security in family and partners, she knew from experience that sometimes those you should be able to count on most were nowhere to be seen.

There was an awkward silence to the room as Taln worked through her thoughts, wrangling herself back under control. By the time she glanced back at Eirse, she was sitting at the computer, and Taln suspected she was trying to look busy more than actually doing anything of significance. Taln tried to open her mouth, to say what she was really thinking and feeling, but the words clogged her throat, refusing to leave. She *wanted* to tell Eirse that if anyone could get her to open up, it would probably be her, but it just didn't feel right.

Maybe the moment was wrong. In the middle of a mission, with the possibility of invisible monsters lurking about, was probably not the best time to express her feelings.

Already regretting her decision, she stepped up to Eirse, retreating back into her professionalism. "I found a few things while you were gone."

Eirse spun the chair around. "I *am* sorry. I wasn't thinking." She looked down and shook her head. "I don't know that you can forgive me, but I never meant to hurt you. You deserve to be happy, and I'm sorry I got in the way of that."

"Eirse, that's not what I meant."

Looking uncomfortable, Eirse changed the subject. "So, what did you find?"

Taln gave up on the idea of explaining. Eirse could be just as stubborn as herself sometimes, and from the nascent expression on her face, Eirse was not going to be moved. "Well, one, they definitely didn't leave."

Eirse nodded. "Yeah, I came to the same conclusion. No comms out for that last erno, and the last of the audio recordings were of screams."

Taln shivered, remembering the death she'd watched. "Yes, I think I saw the attached video. Someone was killed. It was bloody, and there is *no* recording of the creature or person, just a shadow."

"A shadow?"

She nodded. "Even slowed down, that's all I could see. A shadow loomed over the person, then it was as if something with claws went at her, blood everywhere."

"Great Depths," Eirse said under her breath.

"Yeah. Whatever it was, I'm assuming they never figured out how to see it on their security footage." She thought for a second, chewing on her lip. "How did it get in?"

"Good question. And what is it? Is it a native species? Was it one of the subjects they were experimenting on?"

Taln shook her head. "I don't know. Wait." She reached into her back pocket and pulled out the journal again, flipping to the last entry. "Here," she tapped the page. "The person seems to associate the threat with two things. The moon rising and the night."

"Taln?"

"Yes?"

"The moon started rising while I was on the roof."

The both looked behind them at the wall of windows where darkness reigned, a visual reminder that night had arrived.

Even as Taln dragged Eirse's focus back to the mission, the ringing rejection continued to sound off in her head.

You didn't ask how I felt.

You didn't ask what I wanted.

You just took.

It hadn't, not even for a moment, occurred to her that she was doing something wrong. Taln's words made her feel almost like a rapist. She'd taken away her choice, her ability to consent. She'd acted without consideration, with only her own feelings coming into play. It had been an inherently intimate act, and she hadn't given Taln a choice.

I'm a monster.

After that, focusing on the mission was a welcome reprieve. "We should leave."

Taln stopped talking for a moment, just looking at Eirse like she'd grown a second head. "Leave? No. We have a mission to accomplish."

"Clearly, the Diehli is not benefiting from *whatever* they were doing here. The facility was barely established when everything went to the Depths and never resurfaced. It doesn't benefit us to remain here."

Taln shook her head. "I disagree. We don't know how much they interacted with headquarters. For all we know, Diehli Headquarters has every bit of research they did here. Until we've done a thorough investigation, we can't leave."

"So, we just die then."

"No. Quit being dramatic. We are two skilled fighters, and when the time comes, we *will* leave. The people here weren't fighters. They were scientists and lab experiments. They weren't prepared."

"Neither are we. We don't know what we're up against. You said it yourself. This is an unseen enemy. It took out someone without showing up on *any* of the surveillance."

"We don't know that. We know the *cameras* couldn't pick them up. That doesn't mean they can't be seen. Cameras are not the same as the organic eye. They can see things we can't, but we can also see things they can't. We know the people of this facility were scared of these things. We know it's somehow linked to the moon rising and the night. We're also prepared for a fight if need be. If these things turn out to be invisible…"

"We're screwed."

Taln chuckled. "Well, maybe, but we can retreat."

"Not if the shuttle's a three horo hike away."

Taln chewed her lip. "Would you say the cleared area around the building is large enough for a shuttle landing?"

"Well, yeah, I suppose so."

She nodded. "Good. You're right. We need to call the shuttle closer in case of an emergency. If these things really are invisible, I don't want to have to make that trek back through the woods with them on our heels. And holing up in this facility hoping they can't get to us is not an option as far as I'm concerned."

"I think that's the first sane thing you've said."

Taln's face closed down into her standard stern expression before she fell into her thinking pose, one fist pressed to her lower lip and chin. "Now that we know there's a threat, I don't really like the idea of us being here alone. But, we don't know what we're up against, either, so I don't feel comfortable bringing in more people yet. If I underestimate the threat, I would just be leading more people to their deaths."

"All the more reason to retreat. We could wait until the moon sets or until daylight?"

She shook her head. "Then we *really* wouldn't know what's going on here."

"So what? You just want to sit and wait?"

"No, we're going to keep investigating. The sooner we get to the bottom of this, the better." She dropped her hand. "Eirse, are you comfortable going outside, setting a beacon, and calling the shuttle?"

Eirse sighed and nodded. "Yeah. Yeah, I will."

"Thanks."

Eirse nodded and walked away.

Eirse was shaking her head and grumbling to herself as she stepped out of the building and closed the door behind her, conscious that *something* on this planet was dangerous. And she refused to let it get inside and threaten Taln. She might be annoyed with the woman at the moment, but she didn't want her to get hurt.

"This is ridiculous. We should be leaving, not digging in deeper. Practically from the moment we got here, I knew there was something wrong, but did she listen? Noooooo. No, she wants to *investigate* more."

Turning from the door, Eirse took in her surroundings. The moon to her right was big and surprisingly bright even though it was still little more than a crescent over the treetops. Its light cast long shadows across the cleared ground, and suddenly, she was very conscious of the potential threat every one of them posed. "Great, now I'm jumping at my own shadow. Literally!" She pulled out a gun, then brought up the Mission menu on her wrist comm. She selected "Shuttle Beacon." A glowing dot showed up on her HUD, letting her know the beacon was placed. Three options were now on the screen: Remove Beacon, Recall Shuttle, and Back. She selected "Recall Shuttle."

"Perfect. Now we can just wait for the monsters to eat us." Her HUD flashed with a warning. "Shuttle Recalled. Please clear the beacon site."

She walked back to the facility, ready to go inside where there was at least the *illusion* of safety. Being out here was starting to make her skin crawl. Now that she was outside, she realized the moon was the only major illumination out here. They hadn't thought to turn on the outdoor lighting, leaving the entire area in an oppressive gloom that had her hastening her steps and pulling out a second weapon.

She was hyperaware of her surroundings as she crossed the clearing, that big metal door centered in her focus. With each step, she gripped her guns tighter and tighter, her nerves fraying down to nothing as the threat of the unknown loomed all around her. What was worse than being in danger? Not knowing if you were in danger. Not knowing if you would see it coming. Not knowing if you could defend yourself if it did come for you.

Though it felt like an eternity, she reached the door quickly enough and transferred one of her weapons back to a holster to open the door.

The cold metal handle sent chills up her arm, making the entire scene even more ominous and making her that much more eager to get back inside. She pressed downward, automatically pulling at the same time, anticipating the unlocked door letting her in.

Except, it didn't budge.

CHAPTER TEN

aln was working through surveillance data when everything changed. A loud noise, like a thousand deadbolts being engaged all at once, filled the air. The lights blinked out, replaced by red emergency lighting.

Her heart pounded in her chest. She jumped to her feet, filling her hands with weapons on instinct. Spinning around, she looked for a threat, but saw nothing.

"Lockdown engaged," an automated voice said over the building's intercom.

"Lockdown?" she said. "How the hael did a lockdown happen?" She rushed to the computer, but it had turned off automatically or something. It wouldn't respond.

Then a sound unlike anything she'd ever heard before filled the air. It was like a mix between a scream and metal being torn apart. She jerked and spun around to face it as something started to bang on the walls, as if demanding to be let in through solid metal.

She took several deep breaths. "Calm down, Taln. You are a professional. You're armed to the teeth. You can handle anything that comes your way." The little pep talk helped, but the weirdness of the situation still lingered at the edges of her mind, threatening the stoic facade she usually pulled off with little effort.

"Your weapons will do you no good."

Her heart jumped into her throat, and she spun around, her mind stuttering into survival mode as she pulled the trigger.

Eirse cursed under her breath as she pressed her back against the door. The textured metal dug into her skin through her two shirts, but it barely registered. Her hands shook slightly as she aimed her weapons outward.

Suddenly, it was as if she were back in those deep, black, fateful waters. It was dark, and there was something deadly just out of sight. Her instincts had told her, practically from the moment they'd landed, that they needed to leave, but now she knew it without a shadow of a doubt.

This place will finish the job the Vrath started.

She breathed heavily, trying to get a hold of herself. Before her was nothing but darkness and shadow, though. And she remembered what Taln had said. All she'd seen was a shadow and then blood. With night looming supreme over the land, she couldn't hope to escape something as intangible as a shadow.

Then the screaming started. She thrust her left arm toward the noise, which seemed to be coming from the woods.

It was getting closer.

It sounded like some eldritch monstrosity that could drive you mad just by looking at it. She didn't want to see it, was afraid to see it. Her body felt paralyzed as her mind continued to equate this new threat to the Vrath that had mutilated her and killed her partner.

Oh gods, it's coming for me, isn't it?

She was out here, in the open, right where it could reach her. To the best of her knowledge, there was no one left on the planet, and based on the quiet woods from moments before, she suspected the native wildlife wasn't stupid enough to stick around while that thing was hunting.

Eirse holstered one of her guns and checked the status of the shuttle on her HUD. ETA 10 diceros. She cursed again, looking around her in desperation. As the screams grew closer, she knew she couldn't stay here. She couldn't wait for the shuttle. If she waited, she was as good as dead. They would get to her before the shuttle arrived.

But where could she go?

CHAPTER ELEVEN

"Whoa, whoa. Don't shoot!"

Taln didn't lower her weapons, but she did stop shooting. A man was standing in the doorway, hands up in the air as those creatures continued to bang on the walls, making it hard to think. "Who are you? Where did you come from? This is an uninhabited planet, and this facility was empty."

"Well, it was… and it wasn't," he hedged, looking uncomfortable.

She primed one of her guns. "You better make that a little bit clearer."

"I will. Could you lower that, please?"

"No, I don't think I will. I don't know you. I don't know what you're capable of, and there's been a little too much weirdness since this whole mission started. I think I'll keep the guns."

"Oh… okay. My name's Krayvo Ansa. I'm the lead scientist here."

"Then you know what happened here. You know what those things are." She motioned at the wall with one of her guns.

He nodded, gulping nervously. "Yes." His voice cracked. "We call them phasers. They're the reason we're here. One of our company's ships discovered this planet and those creatures. Headquarters thought it would be a valuable resource, and here we are."

"You were experimenting on people."

He paused, taking in and letting out a deep breath, as if hesitant to admit his sins. "Yes, we were trying to port the phasers' ability into sentient beings, allow them to use that ability at will. It didn't go to plan."

"What went wrong?"

"We underestimated how dangerous these creatures were. And we made mistakes, mistakes that cost people their lives."

"What did you do?" She was tempted to prime one of her guns again, shake him up a bit. She couldn't believe the arrogance of this bastard, but he was already pretty shaken. Another threat like that might turn him into a babbling mess, and then she wouldn't be getting *any* answers.

"Well, you see, we'd made some pretty rash assumptions about our research. We'd assumed the phasing could be controlled, but at first, it seemed like nothing was happening. We could confirm the gene had been added, but the subjects just couldn't phase. Then the moon rose, and some phased whether they wanted to or not."

"Phase?"

"Yes. These creatures can become almost invisible and completely intangible, and it seems to work at will, but we couldn't figure out how."

Taln remembered the journal entry. "You gave it to yourself. That's why you're here. You can only become tangible while the moon is out. Why is that?"

"How did you know that?"

She didn't answer, instead hoping her stern expression would keep him talking.

"Okay, fine. Yes, we did. The phasers were about to invade the facility. We couldn't escape. Our only hope was that the gene therapy could work fast enough to allow us to phase, too. Before it was too late."

Taln nodded. "Why the moon? What's the significance there? And what was your mistake? You never said."

"Well, we'd at first thought our research was a total failure, that maybe we'd identified the genes to phase but not the genes to control it. Or that maybe we'd identified the wrong genes entirely. We tried iteration after iteration, tweaking everything we could think of, but the results were always the same.

"Then the moon rose. It was the first time since the facility was set up, and we didn't think anything of it. At first, we just noticed that the animals got very quiet at night. Usually, you can stay up late listening to them, but it was so quiet you could question your own sanity.

"Then there was a commotion from the opposite wing. I ran from my room, through the hub and to the dorms set aside for the research subjects. Several of my coworkers were in the hallway, and all the doors were open. They couldn't find most of the volunteers we'd already administered serum to. Several new arrivals were freaking out, and it didn't take us long to realize it was because people around them had just disappeared. Some managed to come back to their tangible form, even playing with the change back and forth, while others remained unseen all night.

"We were all elated. The experiments had worked. The subjects had phased. We celebrated, but when the dawn came, some of those who'd phased never unphased. We put our heads together, trying to come up with some reasonable hypotheses. The prevailing one was that something, maybe a form of radiation, was emitted by the moon. There was also the hypothesis that the nearest star might be negating its effects. We had no idea what could cause such an effect over so great a distance, but it was the only theory we could come up with."

"What about the ones who never unphased?" Taln said, interrupting his flow.

"Huh?"

"The ones that didn't unphase with the dawn."

"Oh." He sighed, shaking his head. "We don't know. They were from one of the earlier iterations of our research, we know that, but that's about it. There was nothing we could do for them, so we focused on what we *could* do, those we *could* help.

"We sent the shuttle to collect samples from the moon's surface, hoping to find answers. Over the next morgo, we tested those samples. We did find that subjects who'd been administered later variants could phase in proximity to those moon samples when the moon wasn't present, though they still couldn't do so in daylight.

"It was an extremely valuable conclusion, but it came at a great cost. That was our biggest mistake. We weren't paying attention to the world outside of our little oasis here. When the wildlife remained quiet even in the daytime, we didn't pay attention. When we started hearing these unearthly screams in the night, we didn't pay attention.

"No," he shook his head, clearly disgusted with himself, "we didn't start to pay attention until they were right on our doorstep. It wasn't until they started scratching at the walls," he looked over as an especially loud groan of protesting metal pierced the air, "that it even entered our minds. By then, it was too late. I don't know if it was over-predation or if the local fauna had just migrated away, but the end result was a very efficient predator with only one available food supply.

"Us.

"Even then, looking back, I feel like we were especially dense. For days, people had been dying mysteriously, and yet it wasn't until the phasers finally reached the facility that we realized the moon samples were the cause. The prevailing hypothesis was that the phasers could now phase when the moon wasn't overhead and that they'd likely decimated their food supply, making them increasingly aggressive and desperate as they starved.

"We never stood a chance."

Taln relaxed slightly now that she had answers. "How many more of you are there?"

"Not many. It was too late when we decided to administer the gene therapy. Almost everyone died."

"Except the subjects, I assume. They survived."

He shook his head. "Not all of them. The earlier variants had mixed results. Some couldn't phase at all, while others had no control. A few were killed by the phasers in those early days before we realized what was happening. None of them were willing to stay here, though. Not with us.

"Some tried to escape using the shuttle. I don't know if they were desperate or just stupid, but we had to stop them. This planet is too far away from anything. They would have died out in space, far away from any salvation. A few of us followed them, hoping to talk some sense into them, but that's when we found out the shuttle had been destroyed."

"And after that?"

He shook his head. "We were making plans, trying to decide if we should abandon the facility and call for help."

"What did they do after that?"

He shook his head. "I don't know. We never saw them again. We were so focused on figuring out what to do that we didn't even notice when they left. By the time we'd made a decision on how to proceed, a decision I regret to this erno, they were already gone. I assume they're out there somewhere." He nodded with his head at the bank of windows, but made no further comment.

Taln didn't like the way he'd just dismissed their disappearance, but now that her curiosity had waned, other concerns crept back into her consciousness. Eirse was outside setting a beacon for the shuttle. "How do you lift the lockdown?"

"Lift it? Are you kidding? After we just got it up? The lockdown means we can finally unphase without fear of them getting to us. It's the only thing between us and those creatures."

"My partner's out there." She stepped forward, looming over him.

"Well, I'm sorry for your loss."

"She's not *dead*," she snarled.

"She will be. There's nothing you can do."

"Over my dead body! Just lift the lockdown and let me out."

He shook his head. "I can't do that. That'll put you and everyone else in this facility in danger."

"I don't care!" And she realized she really didn't. She didn't care if she was in danger, only that Eirse was, and she wasn't there to have her back.

"You can't fight them!" he shouted back, seeming to grow more confident by the moment. "Your weapons won't work. We learned that the hard way. Even the lockdown is only an imperfect solution. They *can* get through the walls, the doors, the windows, but when the moon is up, they seem to struggle with becoming completely intangible."

"Weapons don't work?" she paused, looking down at her guns.

"No. Until they are actually striking, they're not tangible enough to be hit by any physical weapons."

She lifted one of her guns. "But these are energy weapons."

"I know. It doesn't matter. They're designed to hit physical things."

"Hael."

"I'm sorry. I know how you feel. We've spent every moment we could trying to figure out how to fight these things. I know it's frustrating. Imagine how we felt, with every failure reminding us that we might never leave this planet alive."

"Couldn't you have called for help?"

"When? When those things are out there trying to get at us?"

"No, when the moon's down."

He shook his head. "When the moon's down, we're no more of a threat than they are. We can't touch anything. We need nothing. No food, no sleep. It's like we're in stasis, but we're wide awake. We can move around, but we can't interact with anything. We can plan, but we can't talk to each other. We have no voices." His face fell, and he looked away. "I assume those creatures have some form of alternative communication, something that allows them more than the half-life we experience."

Taln was tempted to say she was sorry, but she really wasn't. These people had done this to themselves. They'd fiddled with things that every modern government said shouldn't be messed with, and they were paying the price.

He turned back around. "You know, we could have called for help. Before the power went out, we could have done it, but there was no point." He laughed and shook his head. "Not when you work for Diehli. If we'd called in a rescue team, they would have died, and we would have been written off as a lost cause. Even if we'd tried to call in a rescue again, no one would have answered."

Again, she couldn't help feeling they'd brought it on themselves, working for Diehli. And yet, Eirse had worked there not so long ago, too. Was she a lost cause? Had *she* brought it on herself? She couldn't be quite so callous with Eirse as she was being with this man and his coworkers. She *knew* Eirse, cared about her. Eirse was a good person. Maybe not the best person, but good nonetheless.

And like the eye in the middle of a storm, a calm came over her. Just thinking about Eirse made the desperation of the situation ease somewhat. The fear, the unknown, was not as important as Eirse was, and somehow that made her feel freer than she'd ever felt in her life. She wasn't worried about professionalism or doing just the right thing. She wasn't worried about making mistakes or not being perfect in someone else's eyes. She wasn't worried about controlling everything. All she was worried about was Eirse, the one person in this great big universe who could actually get her to relax. "I need to get to her. I need to get her back." She didn't mean to say it. It just sort of spilled out, like a building pressure that couldn't be contained any longer.

"I told you, we can't. We can't lift the lockdown."

The phasers outside screamed once more, pounding again on the walls as if begging for attention, as if the people inside could possibly forget them.

"I don't care. You keep saying can't, but it's a bald-faced lie. You can. You refuse to. Are those things dangerous? Yes. Can people die? Absolutely. But I think you forget that everything in life is dangerous. You can't hide from it hoping it'll go away and forget about you. Those things," she pointed at the windows, "are not going away. They'll never go away."

Suddenly disturbingly calm, she leaned forward and spoke her next words slowly and methodically. "If I have to, I will blow a hole in the side of this facility to get to her. The rest of you will be nothing but dead meat. Do I make myself clear?"

He gulped, his face paling visibly. "Yes."

"Good."

Another scream rent the air. Eirse flinched at the sound, an unpleasant reminder that if she didn't act now, it might be too late. She rushed away from the building, heading straight out from the door. Her HUD automatically transitioned to night mode, giving her a clear view of the woods in front of one eye. It wasn't perfect, even a little disorienting, but it was better than nothing.

Fortunately, she was fast. Very fast. The ground was rough under her bare feet, but her long limbs and long, wide feet gave her an edge. In addition, her musculature was designed for moving through water, not air, making them overdeveloped for that task. She ran quietly, trying to come up with a plan on the fly.

The screams died down as she put distance between herself and the facility. Eirse slowed, looking behind and around her. She was surrounded by trees, underbrush, and she could spot a bit of the Diehli shuttle's hull shining in the moonlight.

What could she do?

What might save her?

She could loop around and look for another entrance or possibly an outbuilding, but what if all the doors were locked? What if there were no outbuildings? The beasts' calls had been converging on the facility, and now that she'd run away, she could barely hear them, so she had hopes that if she didn't turn back, she might be safe.

But she wasn't willing to bet her life on that.

She started biting her lower lip, a habit she'd picked up from Taln.

Think.

She didn't know much about these predators. Could they climb? Swim? She looked back at the glint of metal and made up her mind.

There was really only one option. Without more information, there was only one other place that had any hope of shielding her.

The Diehli shuttle.

If she could get into that shuttle, maybe she could survive until help arrived.

CHAPTER TWELVE

fter her brief realization, it was as if the floodgates had opened. Taln couldn't deny it anymore. She cared about Eirse, maybe even loved her. In fact, at that very moment, Eirse meant more to her than anything else in her life. More than the mission, more than her job, more than her own life.

And she's out there all alone, facing those things.

Every time she thought about that, it chilled her to the bone. Taln needed to save her. She needed to get her inside where it was safe. Eirse was the first good thing in her life that felt pure. On some level, she'd never felt secure in her role at Inia Intergalactic. It had always been tainted by her past, by her neuroses. It had always felt like she could lose everything at the slightest mistake, creating this desperate need to be perfect at all times.

And the company had rewarded that trait, seemingly treating it as a strength. Every time she handled a problem with precision because her mind could not accept a single flaw or mistake, she'd been praised. Every time she spent long hours working to make everything just so, she'd been praised. It had reinforced a weakness she'd never had the strength to confront.

Until Eirse.

Perfectly imperfect Eirse. She didn't really know what Eirse was thinking or how she truly felt, but that kiss had spoken volumes. Even though she'd been mad, even though she'd yelled at her, she couldn't deny it anymore. It had felt like coming home, like her soul was opening itself to her other half.

Taln chuckled quietly to herself. She'd honestly yelled at her. She never yelled. She never let her feelings get the best of her like that, always keeping them bottled up inside where they couldn't mess up her carefully curated life.

But Eirse was like a raging storm, and order would always fall apart into chaos around her. She didn't abide by neat and tidy, especially if she didn't believe in the justification for it. Eirse had somehow managed to draw Taln out of her carefully controlled comfort zone, if only for a few moments, allowing her to release what was probably alos worth of emotion.

And now it wouldn't stop. She felt out of control. It made her feel nervous and uncertain, and she wanted nothing more than to reach Eirse, the only balm for what she was feeling right now. She could almost *feel* the other woman in her arms, even though they'd never embraced before. She wanted that right now, almost more than life itself. It was as if she couldn't breathe.

And yet Taln needed her former calm demeanor now more than ever. *Eirse* needed it. She needed to get a hold of herself if she was going to save her. She turned to Krayvo. "You said you've been working on weapons."

He was wringing his hands and sweat was starting to form on his brow. "Yes."

"Do you have any working prototypes?"

"Why?" he said, narrowing his eyes at her.

"Because I intend to go out there."

"You'll be killed."

She stood up taller, trying to pull on her mask of authority once more. "I have my ways. The prototypes?"

"Yes, right. Well, there was a limit to what we could do, being that we couldn't draw power."

"What do you mean?"

He sagged a little before speaking. "Well, it was just dumb luck, really. After taking the serum, and with the moon samples in the vault, we could only touch things at night when the moon had risen. Which is, of course, when the phasers are active as well, so we couldn't go outside.

"Ordinarily, that wouldn't be a problem. The power station should have been in Low Power Mode and trying to use anything that draws power would have taken it out of that mode. But there was a storm, and we think lightning struck too close to the building, forcing the power station into Stasis Mode."

Taln thought back on what she'd read about Stasis Mode. "That can be turned off with an app, can't it? I remember reading that."

He nodded. "It can. If any of your devices have power. The storm happened early in the cycle. Every device, no matter how robust the battery, had died by the time we could phase again. The only things with power left in their batteries were weapons, and those batteries would fry any device that could run the app.

"At that point, all we had left were some weapon power packs and compressed gas canisters. It's a miracle we managed to retrofit anything, really."

"So, what's the problem?"

"The problem is I don't know that they're fully operational. We haven't been able to test them. Not on the phasers, not on each other, not even testing if they'll even fire. Like I said, it's a miracle we managed to even make them at all."

"Hm." She smiled. Sent out into a dangerous situation with no guarantee that her only weapon would work?

Sounds like a party.

"So, might not be able to defend myself. No big deal," she said to herself, forgetting Krayvo was there as she psyched herself up for what lay ahead. *I can do this. I'm not a scientist. I can fight, and if that doesn't work, I can run.*

"No! *Very* big deal. Not being able to defend yourself is *exactly* why you shouldn't go out there. It's not worth the risk."

She thought of Eirse, out there alone and possibly scared. She might even know by now that her weapons were useless. "Oh, it is *definitely* worth the risk."

She turned to him, staring him down. "Show me the weapons."

Taln waited impatiently at the door as Krayvo went to retrieve the weapon. She was on edge and finding it hard to maintain her outwardly calm demeanor. She wanted to rush out into the dark and call out Eirse's name.

You're an idiot, Taln.

What she *wanted* to do was something stupid. Everything inside of her was trying to get her to do something extremely rash and extremely dangerous.

She refused.

If she gave in to her impulses right now, she would probably get herself killed, and what good would she be to Eirse dead?

None.

When Krayvo returned, he was holding a large rifle. She recognized the model and could see where it had been retrofitted.

"Are you sure you want to do this?"

Taln turned to Krayvo, smiling wryly at him. "I mean, what else could I do?"

"You could wait it out with us."

She shook her head and looked over at the door, the same door Eirse had stepped through before the lockdown sealed her outside. "No, I can't."

"Well, here. The gun is based on a standardized model. We retrofitted the firing mechanism and power pack. It was the only thing we could do with no generator at our disposal. There's no guarantee it'll work."

"You've said that already."

"I know. I'm just not comfortable with you leaving. I don't even know if this thing'll fire. And you're the first person who's come here since this whole mess began. If you fail, we'll be trapped here in limbo forever." The gun sagged in his hands as he spoke.

Taln gripped his shoulder, staring him square in the eye. "No, you won't. I have a ship in orbit. If something were to happen to me, they have standing orders to send in another team. If I don't come back, start sending a low power emergency comm. Give them any information they'll need to get in here and leave unscathed. Okay?"

He nodded.

She checked her wrist comm. "They're supposed to rally a team if I don't report in after another nine horos. You can hold out that long. It's not even an erno, and I'm assuming you can phase."

He nodded again. "It's not easy. We don't have a lot of control. None of us have done it very often."

"Well, you're just going to have to try. Just keep yourself safe until I return or my people come in nine horos, okay?"

He nodded.

"The gun?"

He reached out, placing it in her hands.

She accepted it gingerly, staring down at the oversized power pack that felt far too warm to the touch. In a regular gun, that would have been an early warning sign. "Are you sure this isn't going to blow my hands off?"

"Well, of course not. I told you it isn't tested."

She angled a stern expression at him.

"But I don't *think* it will," he hedged. "The power pack comes from one of the turrets upstairs. It's intended to handle a much heavier load."

"And the warmth?"

"Those are always a bit warmer. It uses a different system than handheld weapons."

She touched the various parts, some of them feeling more than a little awkward and flimsy. "And this?" she asked, touching a big, boxy part on top.

"That's the firing mechanism. We had to remove it and add it on top of the gun when we modified it, but we didn't compromise the barrel, so if it misfires, it shouldn't explode." He shrugged. "It was the best we could do with the resources we had. We were just lucky to have an engineer on site."

Taln nodded and lifted the butt of the weapon to her shoulder, sighting down the barrel. She turned to Krayvo. "I would suggest you leave the hallway. Maybe hole yourself up in the hub with the doors closed just in case. I'll be careful, but if there's something on the other side of this door, it could get past me. It would be better if we treated the hall like an airlock."

He nodded and walked away, disappearing around the corner. Taln waited until she heard a door close, then reached for the exterior door. "Here goes nothing."

She opened it and quickly slipped through, pulling the door closed behind her. In a single movement, she had her back to the door, both hands on the gun, and the barrel raised, ready to fire. Everything was quiet for the moment. She pivoted, hoping she might spot Eirse nearby or Eirse would spot her and come running, but an entire dicero ticked by on her HUD without any change.

As she stood there, the darkness irritated her, a constant annoyance that left her feeling a bit awkward. Her HUD, stationed on her right eye, provided the night vision she needed to see where she was going and spot oncoming threats. Unfortunately, that wasn't her dominant eye and aiming through the HUD just amplified the feelings of uncertainty and wrongness she was experiencing.

She waited, getting used to the unusual setup and letting the night settle in around her, letting her pounding heart die down. It was eerily quiet. Even the phasers she'd heard from inside the hub seemed to have died down.

Continuing to monitor her surroundings, she couldn't help feeling unnerved. Everything was so *still*. She remembered walking to the facility. There had been constant noise and movement. Branches and leaves shifting in the wind. Animals calling out or shuffling around nearby. It was organic, living. But now? It felt dead. Even the generator at the other end of the building was too far away and too quiet to be heard from her position. She suddenly worried that when she moved, she would be too loud, that even the brushing of her pant legs together would give away her location to those monsters.

How can Eirse possibly be alive?

Taln shook her head, pressing the gun tighter to her shoulder, using the mild sensation of pain to ground herself. She started a circuit of the perimeter, keeping herself close to the building. Having the entire cleared area between her and danger would at least give her some warning, some ability to react. She hugged the wall as she walked sideways, keeping her gun aimed outward toward possible threats.

Her progress was slow, made slower by her awkward movements and attempts at perfect silence. She half expected her very breaths or heartbeat to give her away sometimes. Her nerves frayed more and more with each moment spent anticipating a confrontation with an unseen enemy using a weapon that might not work.

Time dragged on, made worse by fear and a distorted reality that made it felt like the building would go on forever.

And if that wasn't enough, each of the corners of the building posed their own sort of problem. She had to check the corner without exposing herself, in case there was a threat beyond, but it also meant taking her eyes away from the shadowed woods.

By now, she'd methodically cleared three of the four corners, the last one only a couple arms-lengths away. There was still no sign of Eirse.

Where had she gone?

Had she been at the front of the facility all along and Taln hadn't seen her?

She stopped at the corner and quickly peeked around it, then cursed silently. A high-pitched scream, followed by banging, confirmed what she'd seen. Interestingly, her HUD had shown nothing at all, but from her left eye, she'd seen a shadow on the ground. She *thought* there was only one of the creatures, but it was impossible to truly tell. If there were multiple close together, she suspected the shadows would merge.

She closed her eyes and took a deep breath.

You can do this.

"Moment of truth," she silently whispered as she opened her eyes once more. Lifting the gun, she spun around the corner and fired.

The creature roared and even without visual confirmation, she knew the entirety of its rage was now focused on her. She widened her stance, readjusted her grip, and closed her right eye, pulling the trigger again and again, hoping those reckless scientists knew what the hael they were doing.

Even blindly, she knew the moment it went down. The nature of its vocalizations changed, going from enraged to sort of weak. She heard as it slammed into the ground and slid. She watched as the ghost of its passage marred the dirt, leaving a faint trail behind. *Hael, it must be huge.* Then a hint of blood reached her nostrils, and she wondered if it was the creature's or one of its victim's.

Taln stepped away from the corner, wary of the still shadow on the ground, and continued her circuit, looking for signs of Eirse. But as she reached the door she'd started at, her gut sank.

She let the gun sag at her side, looking out at the empty impenetrable darkness.

Eirse wasn't here.

Where the hael could she have gone?

CHAPTER THIRTEEN

*E*irse ran, not caring anymore if she made noise or if anything was following her. She had a destination in mind, a chance at survival. Branches slapped against her arms and legs, feeling like whips as she ran past. The shuttle was in sight, its hull gleaming in the moonlight. Anticipation swelled in her chest as she grew closer and closer until a loud crack filled the air.

She tensed, eyes and ears attentive, searching for the source. A rustling of branches and leaves. The sound intensified. She looked up and her stomach sank threateningly. A massive tree was falling. She dived backward, and the tree hit the ground like a bomb detonating, forcing her to reflexively cover her ears. Immediately afterward, an excited roar filled the air, and she knew.

They'd felled a tree to try to trap her.

She pushed to her feet and took off, heading away from the shuttle. It was no longer safe. Shrieks and the sound of something big running through the underbrush started up behind her, and she pushed herself harder.

She no longer felt the branches hitting her as she ran. She nearly collided with a tree, but ignored the glancing impact and the throbbing in her shoulder that followed. By now, her feet were numb to the rough terrain, and all that really registered were the sounds of her pursuer and the narrow tunnel of the path ahead.

Eirse had no idea where she was going or what could save her. She only knew she couldn't stop. If she stopped, she was dead. If she stopped, she would end up just like that person from the surveillance footage Taln described. She didn't want Taln to see that. She didn't want Taln to find that. Her throat locked with emotion as she imagined what that would be like. Images of finding Taln on the ground popped into her head, her body torn up, sometimes to the bone, blood everywhere. It would destroy her. She couldn't do that to anyone, let alone someone she loved. She *had* to escape.

But it felt so hopeless, like she was just delaying the inevitable. The only building on this planet was that facility, and it was long behind her. Her pursuer had blocked off the Diehli shuttle and their own shuttle was currently in the air, on its way to the facility. There was no other safety on this planet unless the predator gave up the chase.

Could she run long enough and fast enough to escape it? Or would it keep coming until she dropped from exhaustion?

Eirse stumbled as her feet hit sand. The sudden change in terrain threw her off-balance, and she fell to her knees. Before her, the body of water she'd seen before gleamed, looking majestic, its dark waters still having a silvery sheen to it from the moonlight.

She stared at it, the first body of water she'd seen up close since she left her homeworld alos ago.

I need to get up.

I need to run.

And yet she couldn't. Her limbs felt paralyzed, like the very sight of the water had broken her.

Behind her, the creature screamed, looming ever closer.

Time seemed to stand still, like she was hovering over a precipice and about to fall into the pit below.

I'm gonna die.

There was nowhere left to run. Nowhere to hide. To her left and right, there were just open beaches and before her, a water she had no hope of finding salvation in. She could barely swim. She was certain her pursuer would just rush in after her, grab a hold of one of her limbs, then drag her back. There was nowhere left to go.

Eirse pushed herself to her feet and pulled out a weapon with each hand. She could hear the predator rushing forward, eager to reach and probably eat her. She took a deep breath and waited. "I'm sorry, Taln. We would have been good together. I hope you don't find me." She lifted her arms and aimed at the woods, waiting for the predator to show itself, though as she took in the short expanse of sand, she knew by the time she spotted the beast, it would already be too late.

Oddly, she felt almost like Taln in that moment. Or at least, how she saw her. Eirse was usually a blend of eager mixed with practicality in the face of a conflict while Taln was calm determination. This newfound calm and resignation felt right, like a dedication to the one she'd given her heart to.

She pulled the triggers before she even realized what she was firing at. It was just a shadow, something so inconsequential her conscious mind couldn't even process the significance, but her instincts kicked into overtime, and she started backing up, still firing again and again.

Soon, she was rushing backward, realizing the beast wasn't slowing down, that it didn't even seem to notice her attacks. Her feet splashed into the water, her pant legs soaking up to the knees. The shadow settled on the beach, growling and screaming by turn. She could see it digging its claws into the sand even though she couldn't actually see the claws, only the deep gouges that filled in around them.

Her hips were now submerged, and she couldn't stop firing, even though she knew it was having no effect. Fear hit her hard, but it wasn't just because of the impossible threat in front of her. All her old issues from her homeworld came back, trying to drown her. The scars on her arms and sides itched, and it became impossible to breathe.

Feeling exhausted and defeated, she lowered her hands. What was the point? The guns were doing nothing. The creature continued to inch forward, and she inched backward, step-for-step. In only moments, it would be upon her. Probably only a single leap would do it.

Can I take it down with me?

Was that even possible? The guns had done nothing. What were the chances a knife would do the trick? Even so, going down fighting was better than nothing. She traded her guns for knives and resigned herself to her fate.

"Taln, I hope you find the happiness I never could."

CHAPTER FOURTEEN

Taln scanned the clearing in front of the building, searching for any signs of where Eirse might have gone. Was she alive? Or had the phasers killed her?

She searched the ground for blood, for a dropped weapon, drag marks, anything that could indicate Eirse's fate. She scoured every inch in front of the building, but found nothing. There weren't even footprints, which confused her at first, until she realized she, herself, wasn't leaving any footprints. The ground was too hard and dry. Her panicked brain was just not functioning well enough to realize that.

"Okay. The gun works. There's no sign of Eirse out here. You need to pull yourself together. For Eirse."

It was kind of strange, feeling this out of control for once. She wasn't quite sure how to cope, but Eirse needed her, that much she was certain of. Eirse was out there, alone, without backup. And while Taln had a weapon that could probably hurt them, maybe even kill them, Eirse most certainly did not.

She tried to regulate her breathing, calm her thoughts, but she couldn't bury it all deep like she usually did. There was just too much. They were too strong, and she didn't know how to deal with them. Usually, she just shoved her emotions aside or buried them deep, focusing on the problem at hand. Using ironfisted control, she'd managed to develop a certain confidence about her life and her job, but she couldn't control how she felt anymore. She couldn't bury this and hope it never resurfaced. She didn't even want to.

Taln *wanted* to feel all of this. She wanted to feel a little reckless and out of control. She *wanted* the uncertainty that came with a relationship, especially a relationship with someone like Eirse. All this time, she'd let fear and uncertainty drive her, pushing her to control more and more of her life, shutting down anything even the remotest bit messy. Her employer had rewarded that behavior, but it left her little more than an empty husk of a person, someone who lived in a carefully curated world that never presented any surprises, but also never provided any joy.

"I'm afraid," she whispered to herself, finally admitting the truth, finally letting herself *feel* it. "I'm afraid, and that's okay."

For the first time, the unknown scared her, but didn't paralyze her. She didn't try to run from it or control it. She *wanted* to save Eirse, but there was no guarantee she would succeed. At this point, there was no guarantee she would survive the night. She could be swarmed by those creatures, become overwhelmed and get struck down even with this new weapon. The weapon could misfire, costing precious moments. It could stop working entirely, leaving her stranded far from safety.

This all ran through her head, but her feelings for Eirse were stronger. Her determination was stronger. She had no idea how things would go with Eirse, and she strongly suspected it would be messy. Eirse was her polar opposite in a lot of ways, but she didn't care. Taln might have started out loving her powerful thighs and attitude, but somewhere in the alos they'd known each other, Eirse had managed to smuggle her way into Taln's heart. She'd become someone Taln relied on, even in her cold, controlled, emotionally distant mind and heart. Eirse was the first person she thought of when planning a mission, and for a workaholic like herself, that was significant, because Eirse shouldn't have been her first pick.

On the surface, nothing about Eirse seemed like a good pick for a mission. She couldn't fly a shuttle, knew little about investigating beyond what her security background gave her, had an attitude problem that had her constantly defying authority, and refused to wear shoes even under the most appropriate circumstances. She was difficult to work with. In reality, Eirse should have been the *last* person Taln wanted on a mission, but she wasn't. She never wanted to work without her. She never wanted to *be* without her.

Taln smiled and shook her head. "I'm so dense. I kind of loved her from the moment I first saw her, didn't I?" Somehow, realizing that chased away some of the chaos plaguing her mind. It made her feel happy, possibly for the first time in as long as she could remember. She'd spent her entire adult life trying to prove herself and control everything. Before that, she'd spent her childhood feeling out of place and wondering if her foster parents would abandon her like her own parents had. Happiness was something new to her, and as she stepped forward, moving toward the trees in search of clues to Eirse's location, that promise of happiness helped keep her from falling apart. It motivated her.

"There," she whispered as she reached the trees and kneeled by a softer patch of earth. The ground held the telltale imprint of a Tursiops foot.

She looked up into the distance in the direction the print led. "I'm coming, Eirse."

The predator hadn't moved.

It didn't jump into the water to claw her to death. It didn't slowly stalk closer. No, it just shrieked and growled at her, pacing along the water's edge.

After several long diceros, another slipped out of the trees, joining the first, but it, too, stayed on the shoreline, its shadow never touching the water. A momentary hope slipped into her heart.

Am I safe?

She looked at the two shadows, watching as they shifted restlessly on the sand. Their bulks made fresh divots again and again, those spots filling in as they moved on. "This makes no sense," she whispered, completely baffled. She was so close, she could practically touch them if she stretched her arm out, and yet they stubbornly refused to come any closer.

Were they afraid of water?

She looked down at the water that lapped at her hips. She caressed the silky surface with her hands. It both made her homesick and brought back every insecurity she had. Losing her sails and becoming disabled had caused her to lose her home. It had left her scrambling to redefine herself in environments she was never meant to inhabit. It left her questioning everything she thought she knew about herself. And yet, could the very thing that had caused her so much pain be what saved her now?

She looked back up at the shadows on the beach. They writhed back and forth, and she wondered if it was still two, or if more had joined?

And how long would the barrier of the water keep them at bay? How long until they decided to risk it and test a claw on this medium they'd clearly never approached before?

She ran her hands slowly through the water as she thought. Without her sails, she was a terrible swimmer, but these things didn't seem to want to *touch* the water. Maybe they couldn't swim at all. Maybe they would drown if they tried.

Meanwhile, even if she couldn't swim well, she *could* breathe underwater. Maybe she could wait them out. Taln *had* said something about the threat being associated with the night. Maybe she just had to wait till dawn.

Eirse took more steps backward, the line of the water rising higher and higher on her body until she slipped entirely beneath the surface.

There was a quick moment of panic when her feet slipped away from the ground. She flailed, forgetting for a moment how to swim without sails. She started freaking out when moving her arms about seemed to only cause her to sink deeper and deeper into the water, the light growing dimmer and dimmer. For a moment, she even forgot that her kind could see in waters far darker than these.

But soon enough, the panic washed away, and she got the hang of being underwater again. She couldn't see the shadows on the beach from here, so instead, she focused on telling herself they couldn't get to her.

They don't like water.

They can't enter the water.

As time passed without incident, she began to actually believe those affirmations. She started to feel protected by the water and appreciate it for the first time in alos. She enjoyed the cool, silky balm of the liquid caressing her skin. Her limbs moved languidly around her, keeping her in place with little effort. Her gills effortlessly did their job, making her realize she'd forgotten what it felt like to be underwater. It was different, but it was also peaceful. Sound traveled differently, but she kind of liked it. She liked how the rays of moonlight angled differently, making it feel like she'd left her problems far behind.

"Eirse!" a voice called, the sound wavering as the intervening water distorted it.

Eirse snapped out of her languor. "Taln," she whispered in fear. She looked up, but couldn't spot her. Eirse tried to swim back to the surface, but again forgot how to swim. The panic momentarily resurfaced, but relinquished its hold faster than it had upon first submerging. She slowed down, coordinated her feet and arms, and found that if she spread her toes, she got pretty good propulsion considering her disability.

She surfaced moments later, immediately spotting Taln on the beach.

Right behind the shadows.

With the night vision on the HUD, it wasn't hard to track Eirse's movements. In fact, when she set it in Tracking Mode, all it took was imaging a reference sample, and the HUD automatically lit up any subsequent tracks that matched her footprint.

She rushed ahead, gun in hand, as she followed the bright yellow outlines on the display. There were phasers in the distance, their cries piercing the air, but they weren't close by, and she let that detail slip from her mind as inconsequential.

When she approached a downed tree near the Diehli shuttle, one she was certain hadn't been there before, the HUD momentarily lost the tracks. That fear resurfaced momentarily. She spun around, desperate for a direction. The display only showed flashing yellow letters that read, "Scanning… please wait."

Finally, she looked down around her feet. The ground next to the tree was disturbed, and not from the tree falling. Instead, where her own footsteps hadn't marred the rain-smoothed surface, she could see evidence that someone or something had come through here. There was a spot where it looked like a knee or elbow had pressed into the dirt. Another looked like the folds of a garment.

"Okay, so the tree must have fallen right in front of her. Unlucky."

Or intentional.

Could these monsters be that smart?

Fortified with a bit of knowledge, she managed to pull herself back together again and slowly turned around, allowing the tracking software to do its work.

Suddenly, it highlighted a partial print, and Taln stepped forward. It was the front end of a foot, the heel raised.

Eirse was running.

Taln looked up, and the software spotted the next one. She picked up speed, moving faster and faster so long as the software continued to keep another highlighted print ahead of her.

The tracks led right up to a sandy beach. The sand didn't provide much information other than the fact that *something* had been through here. "Eirse?" she yelled, hoping the woman was nearby and none of those creatures were as well.

She looked from side to side, hoping to see movement, but the movement she saw wasn't what she was hoping for. The sand before her shifted, and so did the shadows tinting it. She lifted her weapon as growls began to fill the air, so close she could practically *feel* them vibrating through her chest.

"Taln! Get in the water! Hurry!" Eirse's voice called from somewhere up ahead.

She looked up as she pulled the trigger, spotting Eirse in the water, illuminated by moonlight, water dripping down her face. A scream that seemed to stab her eardrums pulled her focus back to the task at hand, and she fired again, shooting again and again until the shadows stopped moving.

Mostly confident they were dead, she rushed around the motionless shadow on the sand and approached the water. "Eirse, are you okay?"

Eirse urged her forward. "Get in the water. They won't enter the water."

Taln looked down at the water currently lapping at her boots, then at Eirse, her arms slowly moving against the surface, keeping her afloat. "I came to rescue you."

Eirse smiled, and Taln realized it was the first time she'd ever noticed the woman smiling, and she smiled in return, her chest swelling with happiness.

Eirse shook her head. "Get in here, you hopeless idiot."

Taln shook her own head in answer, her smile morphing into a smirk, then kicked off her boots and settled the gun, which might not be water safe, on top of them. The liquid was cold against her skin as she stepped into the water. She shivered, then rushed forward and dived in, determined to get the shock over with.

A moment later, she surfaced and Eirse was right there in front of her. Taln pulled Eirse to her, cradling her head and holding her tight. "I'm so glad you're safe."

Eirse sighed. "Me, too."

Eirse kept Taln safe through the night, using her comparatively more effective webbed feet to keep their heads above the surface of the water. More of those creatures showed up, screaming and howling, but none of them braved the lake. They all stayed on the sand.

Soon enough, the relief of being together again, of knowing the other was safe, waned, the horos dragging on in a monotonous march toward dawn.

Then the sun finally peeked over the horizon, casting a silver tint to the sky with its blindingly white light.

"I think they're gone," she said, running a hand lightly over Taln's back.

"They are. Krayvo said that, for whatever reason, they're never active in daylight."

"Who's Krayvo?"

"Oh, right. I met him after you left the building. He was one of the people working here for Diehli."

Eirse nodded, then smirked. "Oh, okay. So back to the previous point. They're not active in daylight?"

"Yeah…" Taln said, clearly not sure where Eirse was going with this.

"Sooo… we're alone… in this… idyllic setting."

Taln looked incredulous. "Idyllic?"

"Work with me here."

Taln laughed, but then nodded. "Go ahead."

"And I'm assuming you're not mad at me anymore?" She brushed a finger along Taln's cheek.

Taln clasped her hand gently, holding it there. "Oh Eirse, I was never really mad at you." She shook her head, looking dismayed. "I shouldn't have yelled. You didn't deserve that."

"But you were right. I wasn't thinking about you and what you wanted. I was so focused on trying to express how I felt that the only time I even considered your part in all this was when I was worried you'd reject me." She shook her head. "I was having so much trouble getting up the nerve to say how I felt that action just seemed easier."

"I probably wasn't helping. I wanted to convince myself that if you'd asked, I would have said yes, but I was lying to myself. I wasn't ready. Maybe neither of us was." Taln shook her head, a small smile creeping onto her face. "Why didn't I see it before? Here I was pining over you, telling myself I couldn't have you, and you were probably feeling the same way. How much time have we wasted?"

"Enough," Eirse grunted, leaning closer. "Now can I kiss you?"

"I'd be pissed if you didn't."

"Perfect." Eirse leaned in and pressed her lips to Taln's. It was different this time. The anxiety and fear of rejection leading up to it was gone. She pulled her closer and all their soggy clothes just felt in the way. She moaned as Taln deepened the kiss.

Eirse moved them closer to shore little by little, never breaking contact.

"Too many clothes," she moaned as her hands tugged at Taln's shirts, trying to get access to skin.

"Yes," Taln said, pressing against her even more and hampering her efforts.

Eirse's feet started grazing the ground, and she picked up speed. She wanted Taln under her and on solid ground, where she wouldn't drown if they got too frisky.

When she finally dragged Taln up onto the sand, she pulled back to admire her work. Water flowed around Taln, causing the loose edges of her camo shirt to flap back and forth with the lazy tide of the lake. Eirse smiled. There was something about the water lapping at the woman she loved that had her leaning down to kiss her once more. Nipping at her lip, she pulled back, whispering against the wet pillows of flesh. "I want you naked. I want to admire every inch of your fantastic body."

"Hael. Yes, yes. Let's do that." Taln was actually panting, and it made Eirse's smile grow bigger.

Eirse sat up, knees straddling Taln's hips, and started a slow striptease. She watched avidly as her hopeful lover's eyes blazed with interest, shallow breaths escaping her parted lips, lips just slightly swollen from their kisses.

The camo shirt went first, parting and slipping slowly down her arms. When it was around her wrists, she removed it and flung it at the beach, where it landed with barely a noise. That left her t-shirt. It was wet and clung to her form, accenting her figure. But it also exposed the scars on her arms. She looked down, touching them, suddenly falling out of the moment.

But then Taln reached up, pulled Eirse's arm toward her, and kissed her inner wrist right above the scar. "My warrior," she said with a smirk, and Eirse's smile returned, her insecurities forgotten.

She leaned down and kissed her briefly on the lips, a little thank you, then continued with her t-shirt, teasing the bottom edge with a fingertip and exposing her well-toned abdominal muscles.

Taln reached out, her hands running over the exposed skin as Eirse continued to lift the shirt slowly higher and higher.

"You know," Taln said, "when I first saw you, I thought you were sexy as hael. That confident air, that little hint of danger, and those magnificent thighs that just made me want them wrapped around me."

Eirse laughed and stopped with the lower curves of her breasts playing peekaboo with the air. "I've never been able to get over that ass you have," she admitted. "It just makes me want to grab on and never let go."

"Well then, I hope you do."

Eirse leaned in, hovering over Taln. Her right hand was buried in the sand near Taln's head while her left made Taln's hopes come true, grabbing her firm ass and squeezing just a little. An almost shy smirk crossed her face. "You like that."

Taln's hands moved north, suddenly whipping Eirse's shirt over her head and pulling it down her arms, forcing her to either sit upright once more or collapse on top of her.

"What was that for?"

Taln shook her head. "This is taking too long."

Eirse smiled. "That's my captain speaking." Her smile grew into a massive grin.

"Gods, I want to see that expression on your face for the rest of our lives."

"Me too."

"Now get these clothes off before I do something drastic."

"Yes, Captain."

In the next few blinding moments, they rushed through removing the rest of their clothes. Eirse had no idea where any of it ended up and didn't care. When skin finally touched bare skin, the only thing between them being the water that somehow added an extra layer of sensuality to the experience, she sighed in relief.

She dropped down to rest against Taln, her head cradled by Taln's must smaller chest. "I could stay like this forever."

"It's nice, isn't it?"

"Oh yes." But their calm interlude was interrupted when Taln's hand slithered south. "Taln!" she gasped.

"Just trying to get things moving along."

Eirse moaned this time as Taln's finger found its target, rubbing her sensitive flesh in an experimental pattern that had her shifting restlessly on her lover's lap. "Yes!" she said when the pattern, pressure, and positioning were just right.

Which just encouraged Taln to double down, repeating the move again and again until Eirse was panting and shifting and grinding and squeaking, her body tensing and pulling tighter and tighter. Her mind focused in, narrowing until all she could think about was that release just over the horizon.

Please, please, please.

She lost all sense of the world around her and then broke, her voice piercing the air in a sound that would have put those monsters to shame. She collapsed on Taln, panting heavily as her mind returned to her body. "Great Depths."

Taln tipped Eirse's head up after several moments. "That was beautiful."

"I'm sorry," she said, still a little breathless. "I completely lost myself. I didn't even think about you."

"That's okay. You can make it up to me."

Eirse smirked. "That I can." She pushed up on shaky arms, then slid down lower into the water.

"What are you doing?"

She settled on her knees in the water between Taln's legs. "Making it up to you." Lowering her head, her face dropped below the surface, and she kissed Taln's inner thigh.

"Eirse!" she barked, but didn't move to stop her.

Eirse slowly made her way closer and closer to Taln's apex. She could feel as the muscles in her lover's legs became tenser and tenser the closer she got to culmination. When she hovered right over paradise, she briefly wished she were in the air where she could breathe deep of her essence. With the briefest moment of regret, she leaned forward, taking a slow, gentle exploring lick. Taln jumped against her tongue, and she smiled beneath the water. She did it again, this time using her hands to hold her partner still.

The water no doubt changed the taste, but it still excited her. She could feel the texture difference between Taln's excitement and the water, encouraging her to push forward. The same as Taln had on her, she experimented with different strokes, searching for exactly what her new lover liked, chasing that sensation that would send her straight over the edge.

Before long, she added a finger, too, teasing along her lower lips, testing to see what she wanted. When Eirse's finger ran along the edge of Taln's entrance, Taln moaned, shifting her hips upward, and Eirse took that as permission. She pressed deep, crooking her finger in the hopes that Taln's species had erotic tissue there and that she could find it.

Taln gasped, her entire body tensing and jerking with release.

Eirse sat up, smiling broadly as she watched the always-in-control captain completely lose it in climax. Her body bowed with release as Eirse continued to work her with her fingers, extending her high as long as she could.

"Enough, enough," Taln begged, and Eirse finally relented, pulling her hand away and then licking it seductively.

Taln sighed, dropping her head back against the sand. "Get over here." She didn't even seem to have the energy to lift her arm and motion her forward.

Eirse crawled up next to her, settling in at her flank as Taln stretched out an arm and wrapped it around her. She smiled, feeling self-satisfied as she rested her head on Taln's shoulder. The sun had now nearly cleared the trees, and she closed her eyes to bask in its warmth.

"I love the contrast in our skin tones," Taln said, making Eirse open her eyes. Taln was running a finger idly against her own skin, right where it touched Eirse's. "I love your coloring. It's so beautiful."

Eirse blushed, not really seeing it herself. Her coloring was no different than any other Tursiops.

As if reading Eirse's thoughts, Taln continued, "Yes, you are." She gripped Eirse's chin to force her to see the honesty in her eyes. "You're beautiful."

Eirse shook her head. "No, I'm not. I'm disabled, scarred."

Taln looked down, running a hand along Eirse's scars from hip to wrist. "What, these?"

She nodded.

"Explain."

Eirse shivered at the very captain-y tone, then fell back against the sand, staring up at the gray sky. "It was a hunting accident on my homeworld. I only lost my sails, but my hunting partner lost their life."

"Sails?"

She looked over at Taln. "These scars? There were once sails connecting my flank to my arms. It allowed me to move freely through the water. After that accident, I could barely swim at all. I was useless."

Taln leaned up, hovering over Eirse. "You're not useless."

"I know. I'm not now, but I was then. It took a lot of rein-venting myself to get to where I am now." She smirked, leaning up to kiss the corner of Taln's mouth. "And you helped me get there."

"I did?"

Eirse nodded. "You got me away from Diehli. You gave me an opportunity to do better. You saw something in me that I couldn't see in myself back then."

"Glad to be of service," she said, pulling Eirse in for a hug. "I don't know where I'd be without you."

"Oh, you would have been fine."

Taln pulled back. "No, I wouldn't. I would have been the same shell I've always been. Confident at work but having nothing else in my life. You gave me something more to look forward to. Thank you."

After that, they had no use for words. In no rush to return, they just curled up together, enjoying the new dawn and new intimacy, knowing full well it was only a matter of time before their crew came looking for them.

But they could have this moment.

They *deserved* this moment.

CHAPTER FIFTEEN

When a little too much time had slipped away from them, Taln had insisted they go back. She'd wanted nothing more than to continue to cuddle with Eirse, possibly until they withered away from old age, but they still had a mission to complete, unfortunately.

Even so, Taln couldn't quite get back her normal, "stick up your butt" attitude, as some people were apt to call it. She had the heavy prototype weapon's strap digging into her shoulder and her wet clothes clung to her skin uncomfortably, causing her to chafe in a few places, but she couldn't keep the silly grin off her face or refuse Eirse when she reached out to hold hands. Which they did all the way back to the facility.

The entire time, she was one sly look away from falling into a fit of giggles. It was like she was suddenly the teenaged girl she never really got to be.

And Eirse was no different. Every time she glanced at her, Eirse giggled. Actually *giggled*. She would have never thought the normally tough security officer had it in her. But Taln felt light, like all her cares had been burned away with the morning sunlight. They didn't have to worry about the phasers, she didn't have to resist Eirse anymore, and their mission was all but wrapped up.

But when they arrived back at the facility, everything was quiet. There was no sign of Krayvo anywhere.

"What are you looking for?"

"Krayvo."

Taln shifted the gun's strap on her shoulder, then realization struck her, and she shook her head at her own idiocy. "Of course, he's not here." She turned to Eirse. "He's as much affected by the sun as those creatures are. He's probably here and can't say anything."

"Nine Depths," she muttered under her breath.

Taln nodded.

"Well, what about the mission? How much time do we have?"

Not sure herself, she checked her wrist comm. "About four horos."

"Well, it's daylight. Those creatures can't touch us, and the shuttle's right outside. We could go, touch base with the *Areon*, and form a plan for how to proceed?"

Taln smirked. "Is that really my Eirse? Coming up with a strategy that doesn't involve violence?"

"Hey, I might love a good brawl as much as the next girl, but I'm not an idiot. Trying to do anything here while those things are active is gonna be a pain. The smart choice," she said, rolling her eyes, "is to retreat and create a strategy to investigate when those creatures are out of play."

Taln looked around her, wondering how many people still remained at this facility, stranded and intangible, unseeable, inaudible. What sort of special hael was that? "We need to get these people out of here."

"You mean the employees?"

She nodded. "They've suffered enough."

"But can you trust them?"

She turned to Eirse. "I trust you, don't I?"

Eirse stepped back. "You don't… still see me like that, do you?"

"That's not what I meant."

"Then what did you mean? I don't work for Diehli anymore. Haven't I proven myself?" She laughed, but there was no humor in it. "Haven't I shown I'm not that person?" She shook her head, her hand going to cover her mouth. "I thought you cared."

"I do," Taln said, reaching out to pull Eirse into her arms, but Eirse pulled back, holding her hands out to ward her off. Taln dropped her hands to her sides. "I do. Like I said, I didn't mean it like that. I just meant that, like them, you made a mistake. You accepted employment at a company that was less than reputable. And you regret it."

Eirse visibly relaxed. "I do."

"I'm pretty sure they do, too. So, I want to give them a chance, just like I did with you."

"Okay, but how do we do it? I mean, can they even go anywhere without the moon being up?"

"Yes. They can't touch anything. They can't move anything, but they can move. If we can coordinate with them, then we can create a strategy to get them off-world."

"And how do you propose we do that?"

"They have moon samples in the vault, which can allow them to phase. I know they still can't phase in daylight, but maybe if the vault door is closed? Maybe that'll allow them to phase? If it works, you can monitor us on comms and let us out."

"I guess that could work."

Taln looked around, wishing she could see them. "Krayvo, I assume you heard the plan. I hope you're still in here. Meet me at the vault." She touched her wrist comm. "Sending sync code now."

"Received," Eirse said.

On her HUB, the words, "Open Comm" stayed at the top. She made her way to the vault, a location she'd only passed by without much thought until now. "Now, we just have to open it."

"Might need to head back to the *Areon* after all," Eirse said from behind her.

Taln ignored her, squatting down to examine the lock mechanism up close. She expect Eirse would be right, that they would need to bring a specialist back from their ship if they wanted to open it, but when she got a good look at it, she frowned. The door was unlocked.

She stood up again, grabbed the handle, and pulled it open.

"Well, that's strange," Eirse said from behind her.

Taln turned around. "Maybe they knew the rocks might be necessary for a rescue." *I did* tell them to prepare for a rescue team. Facing the door again, she opened it and stepped inside, waiting and hoping someone would join her.

She didn't know how long she could or should wait. Had Krayvo or one of his coworkers even been in the hub? How long did it take for them to phase once they had proximity to the rocks? Would it even work? With the door closed and no access to real daylight, would that be enough?

She didn't know.

But then it started happening. For the first time, she got to watch the phasing process. It was a little strange, reminding her of a comm fizzing in and out when the signal was poor. And it took a while, the person slowly becoming more and more visible, more and more solid. After a dicero, Krayvo stood before her.

"I'm glad you're here," Taln said.

"Thank you for thinking of this."

"We want to help you get off-planet."

"That sounds very admirable, but we can't leave. Not now."

"Why not?"

"The moon here is the only thing that ever allows us to be our whole selves again."

Taln looked tellingly at the rocks propped on wire mesh shelves, each carefully labeled by size, date collected, and location it was collected from. "Some things can be portable."

He shook his head. "Wouldn't matter. We can't phase in daylight and if we bring these with us at night, we'd get attacked. If *we* can phase with these rocks, so can the phasers. We can't take them with us."

Taln crossed her arms, thinking. "We might not have to."

"What did you have in mind?"

"I see two options here. One, the rest of your staff could also phase here in the vault during daylight." She gestured at him. "I think you've proved that's possible. Then it would just be a matter of getting everyone on the shuttle to go back to my ship.

"Or two, we could take you back when you're intangible. You don't have to be solid to escape the planet. You need to be solid to interact with things. Eirse and I can collect these moon samples here to bring with us or I can send a shuttle to this planet's moon to collect enough samples to allow everyone to phase. Both eliminate the risk. The only downside with the second one is it might take multiple trips. Because we can't interact with you, we also can't guarantee we'll get everyone on the first try."

He nodded. "That could work. But why are you doing this?"

"Because everyone deserves a chance. And that's what I'm offering."

"Then, I'll take it."

Eirse was a bit nervous as they boarded the shuttle. She looked out at the facility, which still looked abandoned, and had a hard time believing there might be a crowd of people around her at that very moment. When she dropped her pack on the floor next to Krayvo, she wondered if the rest of the Diehli staff were standing right next to her, waiting for their chance at freedom.

They'd offered to wait for the rest of his staff to phase in the vault, but he'd declined, pointing out that most of them weren't very good at phasing. So instead, they'd broadcast an announcement that everyone should board the shuttle. Hopefully, everyone was here, but there was no guarantee.

Eirse sat down in her seat up front and waited while Taln ran pre-flight checks. With nothing better to do, she stared at her, wondering if everything would be different now. Were they officially a couple? Would Taln even want a relationship? Or had it just been the heat of the moment?

They hadn't talked about it, instead just sort of going with what felt right in the moment, and now she was a bit worried. She realized that what they did while alone together might not translate to what they would do once they returned to the ship. This could be anything from a one-time fling to a committed relationship, and Eirse was afraid to ask Taln which it might be.

She gripped her seat as they took off, and when they reached space, she had to force herself to stop clenching her jaw.

I'm making a big deal out of nothing, she told herself. And yet, she couldn't decide if she was referring to their time on the beach or her anxiety now.

She looked over at Taln again, tempted to take her hand, but Taln was piloting right now, and she didn't want to disturb her.

When they finally touched down in the shuttle bay, she was again tempted to take Taln's hand, but she held herself back. What if Taln wasn't into public displays of affection? So far, they'd only shown affection when they were alone. What if she would embarrass her if she did that?

And the possibility that Taln would simply set her aside now that they were back? She refused to even consider it. That was a fate that didn't bear thinking about.

Taln threw her harness off her shoulders and stood, turning to make her way to the back of the shuttle, where the doors were already opening, exposing the busy interior of the bay.

Eirse hesitated, but then stood and started departing herself, again staring at the seemingly near-empty shuttle and wondering if it was filled with phased people. She picked up her pack, hefting it over one shoulder, and followed Taln down the ramp as Krayvo peeled himself out of his jumpseat.

They were surrounded by their peers. Mechanics were swarming the shuttle, eager to do an after-mission inspection. At the door leading to the rest of the ship, her coworkers in security filed in, making the space feel even more hectic.

Then all of a sudden, Taln stopped and turned around, her gaze roving up and down Eirse's form. Mind seemingly made up, she stepped confidently forward, wrapped an arm around her, dipped her backward, and kissed her.

It would have been perfect, it would have been romantic, if it weren't for two things. 1: Eirse still had her pack draped over her shoulder. When Taln tilted her backward, the bag threw off their center of balance, sending them tumbling to the floor. And 2: Her coworkers immediately dissolved into hooting catcalls and riotous laughter.

Eirse shoved her pack out from under her and smiled up at Taln, then laughed at the ridiculousness of the moment. A couple spots hurt from her awkward landing on the hard floor, but it felt good having Taln's arm wrapped around her, so she reciprocated, wrapping her own arms around Taln and pulling her in for a proper kiss.

The world fell away and so did her breath. She pulled back after several moments, her entire body tingly.

Taln looked breathless. "Sorry I dropped you," she said once she'd regained her composure.

Eirse's smile grew. "I appreciate the effort."

Taln sat up, offering a hand to Eirse. They stood together, and Eirse yanked the pack back onto her shoulder once more and took Taln's hand. They walked hand-in-hand across the shuttle bay.

When they reached her coworkers, they were waiting in rabid anticipation. "Well?" Xam said, his furry, green bulk crowding her.

Eirse smirked. "A lady never tells," she said as they pushed past them and into the hallway.

Behind them, groans of outrage filled the shuttle bay as her coworkers realized no one was winning the bet.

EPILOGUE

---

*K*rayvo still couldn't believe he'd escaped the planet. He couldn't believe he was tangible once more without fear defining his existence. Tangible and yet safe from the phasers who'd plagued their facility since its inception. He found he couldn't stop touching himself, his clothes, his arms, his face. He'd even gotten into a habit of hugging people for no reason at all. Many of his staff happily accepted the hugs, equally excited to be able to do so.

The *Areon,* the ship run by the woman who'd rescued them, wasn't the largest of ships and housing all of them was a bit tight, but he couldn't care less. None of them could. But that didn't mean the close quarters weren't uncomfortable. These people worked for Inia Intergalactic, a company often derided at Diehli. He'd, personally, always been ambivalent toward them, but on this ship, the same wasn't true in reverse. Many glared at them or looked at them with skeptical glances.

So when he asked for an audience in the conference room, it was at least in part to alleviate that tension he felt between his people and the crew of the ship. But it wasn't entirely selfless, either. He had talked with his people at length about what they wanted to do next. They'd had plenty of time while Captain Taln sent teams down to collect information from the facility that had been their prison for so long.

Most of his staff were pissed and for good reason. They were angry they'd been sent to that planet without a proper plan. They were angry they'd been essentially abandoned by their own company. Diehli had never bothered to check on them, even when they stopped requesting volunteers, even when they stopped sending comms entirely. They were pissed they'd had no choice but to take an experimental gene therapy with unknown side effects. And they all blamed the company they worked for. They were angry. They wanted revenge. They wanted justice.

He couldn't blame them.

Krayvo stepped into the conference room and sat down at the far end of the table, savoring the feel of soft cushions against his back and legs, then waited for everyone else to show up. A few of his coworkers trickled in, people he'd invited knowing they would be the most levelheaded and least likely to turn this meeting into an angry mob.

"What's this about, Krayvo?" Taln said as she walked into the room, looking almost majestic in her uniform.

"We have a proposal to make."

Taln nodded and sat at the other end of the table. "I'm listening."

"I know you work for Inia Intergalactic, and I know that your company has had many less than savory dealings with Diehli, my former employer."

"You could say that."

"So, I'm proposing what I suspect would be a mutually beneficial arrangement. My staff and I," he looked around at the other people at the table, "want to fight back after our ordeal. After a lot of thinking, we realize things like this will continue to happen so long as Diehli exists. We want to change that."

"Do you? I get the feeling you see yourselves as the victims here. I have no problem with people wanting to change, wanting a second chance, wanting to make amends, but what about your own victims? What about your own sins? You were willing to defy the laws of every populated planet in the known universe, and I'm not seeing a lot of remorse here. Did those people even know what you were doing to them?"

Krayvo squirmed in his seat, uncomfortable with the truth. The test subjects hadn't gone in blindly, but looking back, he doubted what information they'd given them had been enough. Diehli was all about results, and sometimes that meant fudging a few details to get past a hurdle. He suspected it wasn't until they'd had to take the treatment themselves that they'd realized the full dimensions of their sins.

And they'd taken it after many revisions had been made. Their "victims," as Taln put it, had no such luck.

"I know. Trust me, I know. We can't change our mistakes. We can only learn from them and, hopefully, try to make amends, as you said. This is part of us trying to make those amends."

Taln nodded, seeming satisfied. "Okay, so what's your plan?"

Krayvo leaned forward onto his forearms. "The Diehli wanted to make living weapons. We never finished our research, and we have no idea how this will affect us in the future. But getting away from the planet, from the phasers, we've been able to practice and get a little control of our phasing." A humorless laugh slipped out of him. "*We* became the weapons they wanted." He stared intently at Taln, hoping she saw the sincerity in his eyes. "I want to use those weapons against them."

"Okay, but how?" Taln asked, looking skeptical.

He took a deep breath. *Well, here goes nothing.* "With your help. If you can get us inside Diehli headquarters, we'll do the rest."

"That's not much of a plan."

"I know, but most of us were scientists." He looked around himself, at the people he'd chosen for this meeting. He thought about all those waiting back in their cramped quarters. "Most of us left are scientists. Most Diehli scientists work at head-quarters, pretty much all of us have, so we know the general layout. And Gharr here can guide us where we need to go to sabotage it. He's an engineer, familiar with the guts of the space station.

"Destroying the station *should* destroy Diehli. Too many of their resources are attached to it. Without it, even if the owners survive, they'll be practically starting from scratch. It could be decades before they could rebuild."

"That station has pretty impressive security. We've gotten into it once before, but we're not going to have that advantage this time. And you'll be going in alone. If they spot you, you're dead."

"Not necessarily. We worked there, at Diehli. We should still be listed as employees. If we just claim we caught a ride after our facility encountered some unforeseen complications, I think they'll accept that."

Taln leaned back, her nails tapping on the table's surface as she thought. "We can't use the *Areon*. It's registered to Inia Intergalactic, and it'll be too easy for the Diehli to get that information. We'll have to get another ship."

"Can you do it? Can you get another ship?"

She sat up straighter and nodded slightly. "I'll see what I can do."

"I brought snacks!" Eirse said, holding up a bowl of puffed grains.

Taln looked up from her captain's seat. "We're not watching a movie, Eirse."

Eirse scowled, a little annoyed that Taln was being such a buzzkill. "Well, forgive me for finding the fun in life."

Taln leaned forward, glaring at Eirse, maybe hoping to cow her into submission.

It didn't work.

"This is not fun. This is a mission. We're here to destroy Diehli headquarters."

Eirse nodded her head excitedly. "I know." She lifted her bowl again, then popped a savory bite into her mouth. "That's why I brought the snacks."

Taln rolled her eyes, but clearly gave up on trying to put a damper of Eirse's excitement.

Eirse plopped down on the seat next to Taln, curling up next to her and offering the bowl.

Taln reluctantly took a piece. "You're lucky this tiny ship has bench seats in the control room."

"I know. It's like it's meant for cuddling."

Taln laughed, but then wrapped an arm around Eirse's shoulders, pulling her in tighter, before activating the intercom. "You all ready back there?"

"Ready and waiting. How long?"

"Just a few diceros. I'm about to contact their flight control now."

"Okay."

Taln leaned forward, not releasing her grip on Eirse as she activated the comm. "This is the *Lover's Nest* requesting permission to dock." She glared at Eirse as she said the name her girlfriend had given the ship.

Eirse just smirked and popped another bite in her mouth, turning her attention to the rapidly approaching space station on the screen.

"*Lover's Nest*, we don't have you on our schedule. What's the nature of your request?"

"Transport. We have a group of your employees on board. We're just dropping them off."

"Their names?"

Taln counted off on her fingers for a few moments, like she was looking something up, then spoke. "I… don't have all of their names. The main person I dealt with was a Krayvo Ansa."

"All right. Let me look into that. Please hold."

The comm went silent as the Diehli employee checked Krayvo's credentials.

Eirse was not good at waiting. "Do you think we could make out while we're on hold?"

"Girl, I swear," Taln said, looking shocked. "It's not the time."

Eirse leaned in closer, nuzzling Taln's neck and cheek. "It's *never* the time. You gotta make time."

Taln leaned into the touch, a small smile on her face as she seemed to forget herself and her responsibilities for a moment. Her grip on Eirse grew tighter, and a small sigh left her kissable lips.

"Okay, *Lover's Nest*, we *do* have an employee named Krayvo Ansa. You may dock."

The two of them jumped apart, and Eirse laughed while Taln blushed prettily and shook her head at her partner, as if scolding her for her antics.

"Thank you. We hear you, and we will be with you shortly."

Taln now fully in "mission mode," Eirse leaned back and watched the screen as the big, ominous space station grew closer and closer.

It was sort of weird watching it from this perspective. Not from the outside like this, she'd done that plenty of times before as an employee of Diehli, but from the perspective of someone trying to end them. It was strange now thinking of them as the enemy when she'd once thought of herself as one of them. Sure, she'd fought against the Diehli plenty of times since meeting Taln and joining Inia, but this was different. Most of those missions involved back-street dealings and fighting against mercenaries and outlaws. But here? This was the very embodiment of the company she'd once thrown her lot in with. *This* was Diehli at its core.

And she had no qualms about what they were about to do. She was eager for it, in fact. She looked over at Taln, who was calmly steering the small ship toward the station, her hands graceful as they swept over the controls.

"Okay, we're docked," Taln said over the intercom.

"Thank you," Krayvo replied. "We owe you more than we can ever repay."

Taln shook her head even though Krayvo couldn't see it. "Some debts aren't meant to be repaid."

Eirse couldn't agree more. Her entire experience with the Diehli had been driven, at least in part, by her need to pay for surviving her hunting partner's death. She'd believed she didn't deserve any better. She'd convinced herself that she belonged there, but none of that was true.

Eirse had never belonged at Diehli. She'd never fit in. She'd *tried,* but she'd never succeeded. When Taln had offered her an out, she'd saved her life. She'd given her a reason for truly living. Eirse looked over at the woman in question, sitting so perfectly upright even though no one could see. Taln had drawn her out, given her opportunity and hope, given her *happiness.*

She only hoped she could continue to do the same in kind and decided there was no time like the present. "Woman, you need to relax." She thrust the bowl into Taln's hands, forcing her to accept, then leaned into her again. "Let's just enjoy the show."

"You do realize I have to undock from the station, right?"

"We have time."

Taln shook her head, but relented.

"How long do you think this is going to take?" Eirse asked in a quieter voice.

"Well, first they have to disembark. Once they do, we can separate from the station. Then they have to move through the station and actually sabotage it. I'm not sure how long it will take. Maybe half an horo, maybe less, maybe more."

Eirse nodded, just enjoying the warmth of the body next to her.

Time passed quietly, and once they undocked, they really did do nothing but sit there and soak in the presence of each other. There was something so calming and peaceful about having someone you loved close by, like all was right with the world and nothing could possibly interfere.

"Hey, Eirse." Taln nudged her in the side.

"Yeah?"

"I think something's happening."

Eirse perked up, her hand automatically going for the bowl of snacks. She watched intently as Taln zoomed in on her controls, bringing the station into greater focus. "Is that a ship?" Her hand went mindlessly between bowl and mouth as she chewed excitedly.

"I think so."

A brief pop of color showed on the screen. "Was that an explosion?"

"Maybe."

Then the comm suddenly broke their focus. "Could really use a pickup right about now," Krayvo said over the encrypted comm channel, sounding out of breath.

Taln sprang into action, quickly docking the small ship, this time, without permission.

No one tried to stop her.

Eirse noticed more ships leaving the station.

"Ready when you are," Taln said.

"Okay, we're at the doors. Open up."

Eirse waited impatiently as more ships seemed to abandon the station, and Krayvo gave them the go ahead to depart. Her excitement made her want to jump and *do* something, but there was nothing to do.

What had they done?

What was about to happen?

She couldn't take the anticipation.

Taln rocketed the ship away. But Eirse wasn't willing to give up her view of the station, so she reached over, pressed a split screen button on the console, and selected the rear view cameras. It now looked like a cloud of shuttles and ships surrounded the station. A moment later, the station exploded. She shrieked, dropping her bowl of snacks and jumping up in her excitement. Little bits of seasoned grains peppered the control room floor as she jumped up and down in her glee. "Yeah!"

"You are cleaning that up," Taln said as she continued to fly them to safety.

"Sure, I don't even care at this point. That was awesome." She'd never seen a space station blow up before. It was both spectacular and a little underwhelming, being that flames couldn't survive in space. She collapsed back down on the bench seat and sighed. "Mission complete."

Taln looked down at her and smiled. "That it is. Now there's only happily ever after."

She smirked. "At least until the next mission."

Taln shook her head. "You and your violence. What am I gonna do with you?"

"Love me, of course."

She leaned over and kissed Eirse on the forehead. "Yeah. Yeah, I'll do that."

"Me, too."

A new series is beginning in 2023. Get started with Justine's story in Matched to the Alien Prince.

For Justine, nothing short of leaving Earth will ever make her feel safe again, so she signs up for an interstellar matchmaking service. But will her "ideal" match help her heal, or will his secrets break her trust for good?

Pre-Order Now

GET 2 FREE EBOOKS

I love building relationships with my readers. As part of that, I regularly send emails with deleted scenes, never before seen excerpts, pre-order and new release announcements, and more.

If you sign up to receive these emails, I'll send you <u>Mila's Flight</u>, the prequel to the Darkest Day series, and <u>Shifting Sides</u>, the prequel to the A Shift in Space series, FREE.

Join Now to Get Your Free Ebooks

www.theeternalscribe.com

Danielle

ABOUT THE AUTHOR

Danielle Forrest is a Paranormal SciFi author and Medical Laboratory Scientist based out of Indianapolis, IN.

She has dedicated her life so far to two things:

Science & Books

So it really shouldn't be a surprise if science finds its way into even the most fantastical examples of her writing.

Sign up for her mailing list at www.theeternalscribe.com to get access to exclusive content and updates.

facebook.com/theeternalscribe

twitter.com/theternalscribe

instagram.com/theeternalscribe

goodreads.com/theeternalscribe

amazon.com/author/danielleforrest

bookbub.com/profile/danielle-forrest

ALSO BY DANIELLE FORREST

THE DARKEST DAY SERIES

Mila's Flight

Mila's Shift

Tristan's Choice

Terra's Fate

The Darkest Day Collection

A SHIFT IN SPACE SERIES

Shifting Sides

Shifting Cargo

Shifting Loot

Shifting Paradigms

Shifting Tides

Shifting Shadows

MATCHED TO THE ALIEN SERIES

Matched to the Alien Prince

* 9 7 8 1 9 5 0 7 9 5 1 8 5 *